I0687057

Lost on the Road to Love

by

Kay Harris

I Want Morrison, Book Two

Lost on the Road to Love

Cover Art by *Kristian Norris*

The Wild Rose Press, Inc.
PO Box 708
Adams Basin, NY 14410-0708
Visit us at www.thewildrosepress.com

Publishing History
First Champagne Rose Edition, 2018
Print ISBN 978-1-5092-1995-7
Digital ISBN 978-1-5092-1996-4

I Want Morrison, Book Two
Published in the United States of America

I rested my hand on my hip.

"Are you saying you find me irresistibly attractive?"

"Yes." He gave a firm nod. There was no mirth in his eyes or in the set of his mouth.

I narrowed my gaze and scrutinized him. "I thought it was because we're so close, remember."

"Yes. *And* you're insanely hot."

"Am not!"

"Are too!"

I shook my head.

"Wanna make a bet on it?" he challenged.

"What?"

"You get naked for me. And if I am disappointed, you win the bet. If you're as hot as I think you are under those clothes, I win. In fact, I already know what I want if I win. I want to see one of the films you've made."

I stared at him, my mouth agape.

"What do you want if you win, Chels? Not that it matters. Because you won't win."

I finally found my voice. Because I couldn't turn down this opportunity. "If I win, you sing for me."

"Done." He settled farther into the couch. "I'm ready when you are."

Dedication

For Jim.
You are my travel companion,
my adventure partner,
and my heart.

Chapter 1

Present Day—San Francisco, California
Chelsea

I bounce up and down on my toes trying to warm up. The late October wind has me chilled. I feel like a complete ass as I knock on the door. And when my brother opens it and I see his face, the tear hovering at the edge of my eye falls. It creates a damp track down my cheek.

"Chels, what's going on?" Jack asks me as soon as he takes in my disheveled appearance on his doorstep.

I don't really answer. I'm too busy swallowing back the pain in my chest. So Jack pulls me into the apartment and shuts the door behind us. He puts his arm around my waist and walks me to the couch. "Hey, Candie. Baby, can you come in here?" he calls toward the back of the apartment as he settles on the couch with me and wraps me up in his arms.

I tuck my head into Jack's chest and take a couple of deep breaths. The soft padding of Candace's feet sounds across the hardwood floor.

"What's going on?" my sister-in-law asks from the other side of the couch.

"I don't know yet," Jack tells her.

"I'll make some tea." Candace walks away from us, toward the kitchen.

My brother rubs my upper arm gently and kisses the top of my head. And I know I've come to the right place. I couldn't be alone with my hurt anymore, and since I couldn't turn to my best friend, Jack had been the first one to come to mind. And even though I'm still in a lot of pain, I feel better already. Because Jack will know how to fix this, how to fix me.

Candace returns to the living room and sets a steaming mug on the coffee table in front of me. Then she sits on the edge of the chair across from us and folds her hands together, her forearms resting on her knees, her eyes filled with concern.

I take in her perfectly curvy figure, her creamy dark skin, and her magnificent face. If I looked like Candace, things might be very different for me. But I don't. I look like my brother Jack, except instead of being filled out and graceful, I am slim and awkward. Where the light skin and blue eyes are amazing on Jack, they make me look like a refugee from a northern island with no sun. And where Jack's height makes him seem regal, mine makes me look a Gumby doll.

But I don't envy them their appearance. I'm happy with who I am, most of the time. What I envy is their happiness.

Candace gives me a sad smile. "Are you all right, sweetie?"

Her concern is genuine, her compassion like a warm blanket over my shoulders. "I'm so glad you married my brother," I tell her.

She smiles at me. She knows I think the world of her. "Me too," she says, her eyes glancing up at Jack for just a split second before looking back at me. "That's how I got you as a sister."

Jack squeezes my arm gently. These two people love me intensely, and that is exactly why I came to them with my broken heart.

I wipe at my eyes and sit up, reaching for the mug in front of me. "I suppose you guys are wondering what I'm doing here."

"Yeah, actually, we thought you were supposed to be headed to LA this weekend," Jack says.

I nod. "I'm supposed to be there right now. In fact, I'm probably going to get fired over this."

There is deep silence in the room for a moment. Then Jack does what he always does; he finds the silver lining. "Well, that's okay. I mean, the show was going to be done anyway, right?"

"Yeah, but it was a hit, and I guess I can kiss next season goodbye."

"What happened to make you leave your job?" Jack asks.

"I can guess," Candace says. We both look up at her expectantly. "The same thing that made me leave mine once. A man. Am I right?"

I nod.

"Oh shit." Jack flops back in the couch. "Not—"

"Yes, him," I say.

"I thought you were just friends."

"You are so naïve," Candace tells her husband.

"Well, what happened?" Jack asks me.

I let out a heavy sigh. "It's a long story."

Candace tucks one foot beneath her butt and leans back, her mug of hot tea cradled in her hands. "I think you better start from the beginning."

****

Eight months ago—Los Angeles, California

He walked into the room. The scene unfolded in slow motion. He moved fluidly. Long legs clad in worn jeans carried him through the doorway. His T-shirt, which sported a faded band logo for the rock group Chrome, molded itself to a muscular chest and sculpted biceps. His strong chin was covered in a dark five o'clock shadow that matched the eyebrows above his chocolate brown eyes. His face was framed by long, perfectly straight, glossy black hair that tucked behind his ears and hung down below his wide shoulders.

My mouth went dry, my eyes involuntarily widened, and my body became completely still. He was even better looking in person than I'd imagined.

"Henry, good to see you," my boss, whom I referred to as Snarky Steve, said in a surprisingly generous tone. He even rose from his seat to shake the man's hand. "Please have a seat."

Henry Rushton folded all six foot four inches of his lean, muscular build into the chair next to Steve, which put him directly across from me. I tensed as his eyes swept the room and landed briefly on me before continuing to my right. I watched closely as he took in his new companions, his face perfectly smooth, never betraying a single emotion.

"Let me introduce you to your crew," Steve said. "They'll be with you every step of the way. This is Rodney, your director, and his assistant, Gerry." He gestured to the stern, balding chauvinist I'd had the misfortune of working with in the past and his boney, pasty assistant. "And this is Chelsea. She'll be working the primary camera, and Tom will be doing secondary shots, sound, and editing," he said, quickly motioning to me and the one person in this entire working group I actually liked, the near-retirement malcontent sitting beside me. Henry's eyes landed on me again, only this time they lingered. I could feel the heat rising in my cheeks.

This sensation of helplessness in the face of such an all-consuming attraction was the ultimate result of one fateful day ten years ago. I'd been a geeky, underdeveloped teenager with frizzy hair and unfashionable glasses. Boys paid absolutely no attention to me unless it was to tease the crap out of me. And up until then, I'd had no interest in them. But then I'd picked up my brother Hayden's music magazine on a Sunday afternoon, and I'd instantly suffered my very first crush right then and there.

It was the first picture anyone had seen of Henry since he was just a baby. The caption read, "Henry Rush caught coming out of a concert with his famous father." I'd been immediately intrigued by the tall, thin teenager with strong features and mahogany eyes.

I learned his name was actually Henry Michael Rushton. His father was a famous rock star who went by Sean Rush, but whose real name was Sean Rushton. As a result, he'd passed his real name onto Henry, but the media never did catch on to it, and they always referred to the prodigal son as Henry Rush. Furthermore, I'd found out that Henry was named after another rock star, his dad's best friend Henry "Hank" Tolk.

Despite the fame surrounding him, it was the fifteen-year-old boy I'd seen in that magazine that I was truly interested in. But there was very little information available about him other than his name and age because his parents had guarded him heavily from the media his entire life. So I'd followed his father's long and storied career instead.

"We've given you the best of the two crews, Henry," Steve was saying. "They will shoot all your scenes as well as the ones that you do jointly with Tyressa."

"Hmmm" was Henry's only response.

"I thought we'd go over the tentative schedule. We've left some wiggle room in it so we can make changes as the season progresses. Since the show will start airing before we're done with the entire season, we can stay on our toes and respond to audience reaction," Steve said.

Henry looked skeptical about the schedule as he watched Steve pull it out of a folder. In fact, he looked skeptical about everything. I couldn't blame him. This really was a bit of a hair-brained scheme, even for our fledgling cable channel staffed almost entirely by multiple-failure second-rate show execs and the starry-eyed millennials they'd talked into taking low-paying jobs for them—like me.

I'd taken the job with Trek straight out of college. The director I'd done my internship under had gotten me the gig, and I was grateful. Really, I was. Because I worked for a travel channel, I could live in my hometown of San Francisco instead of having to move to LA, since almost all of my work was done in offsite locations anyway.

I liked the work. While my ultimate goal was to direct films or produce shorts, I was young and learning, so running the camera was a good start. And I enjoyed the travel. Thanks to my job, in the last four years I'd been all over the world.

So when I got called about working on this show, I figured it would last at least a few months before it got scrapped, but I could rack up a few more killer locations. The premise, to have the children of famous people show off different sides of various vacation destinations, was almost as stupid as the name, *Next Gen Adventure*. They planned to get a male and female counterpart of famous brats for each new season. As if there would be more than one.

It was dumb, but a job was a job, right?

And then I'd heard about who'd they'd gotten to do the first season of the show. Henry Rushton was to be the male side of the kid fame duo. His partner would be Tyressa James, the daughter of actor Roger James, who was known for a series of action films he made after first becoming famous on a television series where he played opposite Henry's aunt, Stacey Rush.

"So we won't stay in LA long. We'll be leaving tomorrow for New Orleans," Steve was saying. "But we will be returning. And since both you and Tyressa are from LA, we'll be doing, at the very least, a homecoming episode here."

Henry nodded.

"So, um, is the hotel we've put you up in okay? I understand you flew in from San Francisco last night?" Steve asked.

My ears perked up. Henry lived in San Francisco? I wondered how long that had been going on. I knew he'd grown up in Malibu and he'd gone to college at UCLA. But now he was living in *my* town?

"I didn't stay in the hotel," Henry told him. "My mom would have thrown a fit."

Steve flinched from the effort of suppressing the

snarky curl of his lip. He truly believed everyone under the age of thirty was a loser who lived in their mom's basement. So I'm sure Steve didn't think much of Henry crashing with his parents while he stayed in his hometown. I, however, thought it was both perfectly normal and highly adorable.

"Okay, well…" Steve rubbed his hands together. "We'll start with a brief scene at the Biltmore in the morning before getting on the plane. Tyressa and her crew will be there as well. You've met Tyressa, yes?"

Henry let out a breath. His cheeks puffed up, and his lips separated. "Yeah, I've known her since we were kids."

"Of course, of course," Steve said, nodding his head.

Steve had not done his homework about the costars. But I wasn't surprised. He hated this gig. It wasn't his idea at all. It was his boss's idea. And he could have given two shits about these coattail kids, as he'd referred to them last night when we first met as a team. So, of course, he didn't realize Henry and Tyressa would have known each other nearly all their lives.

Steve also didn't buy into the concept for this show at all. But the channel's vice president, Ken Atlas, was over the moon with this idea. He was convinced the show could bring a younger audience to the channel. And he figured by starting the show's first season with the son of a legendary rocker and the hot daughter of a notorious actor, he had gold.

What I wondered was how the hell Ken had talked Henry into doing it. This guy had stayed out of the spotlight his entire life, and he'd shown no inclination to change that as an adult. He'd kept his head down all through college and after. I was sure of that because if Henry had been out in the public before now, *I* would have noticed.

Or maybe not. After all, my childhood crush had gone dormant when I couldn't fulfill it with more pictures and news. And I'd eventually learned real men could be a lot of fun. I was a geek all through college, but I wasn't alone. It wasn't socially crippling like it had been in high school. So I'd had my fair share of boyfriends, flings, and friends with benefits. In fact, the phantom crush might never have reared its head again if I hadn't come face to face with the man himself that very afternoon.

"Well, Tyressa said she was very happy to be working with you. I have no doubt that this show will be a big hit," Steve said, big salesman-grin in place.

Henry nodded stoically. And I could see Steve getting nervous. If Henry was as quiet as his famous father was known for being, getting him to be a vibrant on-screen star was going to be like pulling teeth.

"Okay, then. I guess we'll meet up in the morning." Steve clapped his hands together.

Henry stood. Tom and I followed suit. As Henry turned toward the door, I moved around the table, trying to get closer to him. I wasn't sure exactly what my plan was, I just didn't want to see him go without saying *something* to him.

My anxious feet moved across the carpet until I was right behind Henry. He moved through the door, and I managed to slip out behind him. Then, speeding up, I got right beside him as he made his way to the elevator.

I still didn't know what to say, and when he

stopped in front of the elevator and hit the button, I stood mute beside him. Then he turned and looked right at me.

I was a tall woman, but I was still about six inches shorter than Henry. His head tipped down slightly as he looked at me. It gave me a great view of those dark brown eyes, and I was instantly lost in them, just as I'd been at fifteen.

"Chelsea…Chelsea Morrison?"

Chapter 2

I blinked. My mind went from blank to whirring in seconds flat. Henry Rushton had heard of me? I mean, yes, most people in California knew of my family and by default, me. *But Henry Rushton knew me.*

"She is," Tom said, his voice coming from somewhere to my right. I wasn't entirely sure where because I wasn't capable of actually ripping my eyes off Henry to find out. "And she's the best damn camera operator this two-bit channel has ever seen."

"Hmmm" was Henry's only response.

I felt Tom elbow me in the ribs, and I blinked, trying to focus. It didn't work, and I remained silent.

"She's usually not so quiet," Tom said. I managed to turn my head so I could see his furrowed brow as he stared down at me. "She's..." He shrugged, then looked back up at Henry. "She's great, though."

I thought about talking. I really did. But I just couldn't do it. What on earth could I say to the man who had stolen my teenage heart with just a picture? As I turned back toward Henry, I used my forefinger to push my glasses up on my nose. And we stood there in awkward silence. Fortunately, it was broken by the *ding* of the elevator followed by the opening of the doors.

"Nice to meet you both." Henry tipped his head in a brief nod before slipping into the elevator.

"What the hell was that all about?" Tom asked,

turning me by the shoulders.

I looked down the hall to see Gerry headed our way and pulled Tom into the stairwell so we wouldn't be overheard. A fit and active sixty-eight-year-old, he easily kept up with me as I climbed the four flights of stairs in the hotel from the conference room we'd met in to my own room on the sixth floor.

I pulled Tom into my room, shut the door behind us, and collapsed on the bed. "Holy shit!"

"What the hell is going on, Chels?" Tom asked, moving to stand in front of me.

I sat up and looked at him. He was the only person in the world outside my family who I let call me "Chels." Other than Tom, it was reserved exclusively for my brothers and father. But Tom and I had grown extremely close in the last four years since I started working for Trek. We'd toiled away on a lot of the same assignments for the network. And we both lived in San Francisco. Tom and his husband, Tim, were good friends with my sister-in-law's parents, and their son, Brian, worked for my brother, Jack. Our lives intertwined, and when I traveled with Tom it felt like having a family member around.

"This is really embarrassing," I said, running my hand through my hair. "But that was my first crush."

Tom smiled. "That's pretty adorable."

"Not adorable. Pathetic," I protested. "And embarrassing as hell. I was a complete disaster!"

Tom's deep throaty chuckle shook his ample belly. "Everyone has a childhood crush, sweetie. I tell you what. If I'd come face to face with Burt Reynolds, you would have been picking *my* jaw up off the floor."

"How am I going to work with him?"

"You've known about this for two weeks now. One, I can't believe you didn't tell me. And, two, you should have been more prepared."

"I didn't think it would be such a big deal. I was fifteen, and I had a crush on a freaking picture of the dude in a magazine. But when I saw him in person…all grown up….Jesus."

Tom slapped his hand on my shoulder. "He's a looker, all right. I think we better go get a beer."

I looked into his kind green eyes and nodded. "Good idea."

****

In addition to being beautiful, Tyressa James also happened to be arrogant, rude, and completely vapid. And apparently, Henry already knew this. He stood beside her on the lawn in front of the hotel, his eyes focused on some point in the distance as she talked at him. Despite being busy setting up the shot, I still heard everything she said.

"I think this is going to be soooo fun, Hank!" In March in LA and under sixty degrees outside, she wore a tiny skirt and cropped top. It showed off all her ample assets.

"Tyressa, you are not going to call me Hank for the next several months." Henry turned and pierced her with his gaze. "I've been telling you since we were kids—my name is Henry. Hank is my uncle."

"But Henry. That's such a stuffy name. Our audience will relate better to a Hank." She put a hand on her curvy hip, which thrust out her ample, barely covered bosom. Through the lens of my camera, I watched Henry sigh heavily and turn away from her. "It's edgier. Or least less dorky," she continued. "And I think you should consider being called that on camera."

"No," he said tersely.

Tyressa looked around her for a minute. Then she dropped that subject altogether and brought up a new one. "I'm glad I have you, Henry. I mean, I'm the only woman on this entire set. At least I have you as a friendly face."

I was used to being discounted on the set. Most of my male coworkers either thought of me as just one of the guys or didn't take notice of my existence at all. In fact, the only people who ever seemed to take note of my gender were the men I slept with.

Henry looked right into the camera I was focusing. "No, you aren't."

I froze, keeping my face behind the equipment as Tyressa followed his gaze right to me. "Oh, right, the camera girl. She doesn't really count."

Henry crossed his arms over his chest and turned toward her. "And why wouldn't she count?" I wasn't sure if I imagined it, but he sounded pissed off.

"I don't know. She's...she's a cameraman. I mean...and she's kinda..." She looked me up and down blatantly, which was made all the more awkward by the fact that I stood no more than a dozen feet away. She took in my jeans and hoodie ensemble, which in my opinion was way more appropriate for the early spring day than her little summer fun outfit. "Boyish," she finished.

That was it. This was just getting weird. I stood and looked at them both, my hands on my hips. "I'm right here, you know."

Henry looked at me and grinned but didn't say anything. For some reason, I felt like I could read him. I sensed challenge in that smile.

"Sorry," Tyressa said petulantly.

"I'm boyish, am I?" I asked.

I heard Tom make a noise, and I knew a chuckle had escaped his throat as he listened in on this conversation. He was always highly amused when I got my attitude on.

Tyressa shrugged. "A little bit, yeah. You a lesbian?"

"Maybe," I said casually.

"Yeah, I figured," she said, looking down at her hands as she played with her fingernails.

At that point I just wanted to play with her. So I did. "What was the giveaway?" I stepped out from behind the camera. I watched Henry closely. One eyebrow was raised, and his lip curled up on one side. I suspected he knew my game.

Tyressa looked me up and down again. "Sandals *with socks*, jeans, baggy sweatshirt."

"But the jeans fit her so well," Henry said in a low, husky voice.

I shivered.

"Hmm, I guess," Tyresssa said. "But then there's the hair. You clearly couldn't care less about it."

That was unequivocally not true. I had fought a twenty-five-year battle with my hair, and it finally looked halfway decent these days. The frizz had turned to light, bouncy curls that hung around my shoulders and framed my face. The natural strawberry blonde color had taken on a darker hue in the last few years that made it look more like raspberry jam than pumpkin pie. I was pretty damn happy with it.

But I tossed it away from my face as if dismissing

it. "So true."

"And are you even wearing makeup?" she asked.

I was actually. I wore mascara because otherwise I looked like I had no eyelashes, and I'd also put on my favorite pink lip gloss that morning. "Who could be bothered with such things," I said airily.

"See," she said, waving her hand dismissively at me.

Before I could launch into a diatribe I knew I should not unleash on this stereotyping asshole because she was the talent and I was the lowly camera girl, Henry did it for me. "So that's what a lesbian looks like, eh? Because my Uncle Al's sister-in-law would blow your little theory out of the water."

Tyressa rolled her eyes. "Here we go. I forgot you and your whole family are all crazy PC all the time."

"You know what? I'm not going to waste my time talking to you, Tyressa," he said angrily. "Can we get on with this?" He turned to me. "Where's Rodney?"

I shrugged and headed back behind my camera. "I'm ready."

"Me too," Tom called.

"Rodney!" Tyressa shrieked.

Rodney climbed out of the van parked behind us, running a hand over his ample belly. "Hey, you set to go, Chelsea?"

"Yep," I said, suppressing the snarky response I wanted to give. What part of me hunched behind my camera didn't say ready?

"Okay. This is super simple. We just do the show intro here. You guys have seen the script and memorized it?"

"It was only two lines," Tyressa said snottily.

Henry just nodded.

"Good. Let's go."

Six takes later, we'd bagged the intro, which consisted of Henry saying, "It's time to explore new places, meet new people, and experience new things," followed by Tyressa saying, "This week on *Next Gen Adventure!*"

Despite the fact that Henry clearly disliked being on camera, being near Tyressa, listening to Rodney bark, and possibly even talking at all, he pulled off his line flawlessly on all six takes.

"That was great. Did you take lessons from your aunt?" Rodney asked Henry, slapping his back as they walked past me and Tom.

"No" was Henry's only response before ducking into the van that would take our crew to the airport.

Tom and I packed up the equipment and slipped inside. I ended up sitting directly in front of Henry, who, instead of going back in the limo with Tyressa, had taken the very back seat in the van. Tom sat on the bench seat beside me, Rodney was in the front passenger seat, and Gerry drove.

The van headed into LA traffic, and I stared out the window, hyperaware of Henry just a few feet away. We were on the freeway, an Eagles tune playing on the radio in the background, when I felt a hand on my shoulder. My entire body stiffened.

"So, camera girl, you appear to be full of spitfire," Henry said in a rich, caramel voice.

He'd leaned close to me. I could feel it. And my hair moved just the tiniest bit when his breath caressed it. Jesus, this childish crush thing sure felt real.

"I can't stand haters, that's all," I said.

His hand slid off my shoulder, and he leaned back in his seat. "Me, neither."

****

Seven months, three weeks ago—New Orleans, Louisiana

"Come on, Henry, look alive!" Rodney encouraged.

"I don't know what you want me to say about this place," Henry said.

"It's supposed to be the hottest night club in the city. Surely, you can find something to say," Rodney coaxed.

They were standing in front of the club, a line of people waiting at the door behind them. They'd spent the last ten minutes squabbling about what Henry was going to say about the club while Tom and I set up the equipment.

"You weren't in there long enough. Maybe go back in, have another drink. We'll get some more B-roll and do this segment afterward," Rodney suggested.

I knew that would be a lost cause. Our B-roll consisted of Henry drinking a local beer and shooing away everyone who approached him. The best shots I got were of the crowd around him and did not feature Henry at all. It would be no different if we went back in. Henry clearly did not do nightclubs.

"I'll think of something to say," Henry grumbled. "Just roll."

Rodney looked skeptical, but he stepped out of the shot nonetheless.

I watched Henry through the camera. He looked great in a pair of jeans and a black cotton button-up shirt. It was what he'd chosen to wear after rejecting the outfit Tyressa's stylist, Kimberly, had picked out for him. I hadn't gotten to see it for myself since Henry arrived at the vehicle after dinner wearing exactly what he had on now. But he'd complained about it in the back of the van. Apparently, it had involved pants so tight there would never be any grandkids for his mom and a silky rainbow-colored shirt.

"All right. Roll it, will you, Chelsea? I'll just figure it out as we go," Henry said to me.

I turned to Rodney, expecting him to protest. But he just waved his hand in defeat. So I rolled the camera.

"While Tyressa is on a historic tour of the great city of New Orleans, I'm exploring the bars and pubs of the French Quarter," he began. "The two sides of this city are illustrated beautifully..." With enthusiasm and a light in his beautiful, dark eyes, Henry went on to expound upon how the city's nightlife provided entertainment to visitors.

I was so deeply impressed by how he was able to talk so eloquently about something he obviously wasn't interested in, I didn't realize it when Henry finally finished speaking.

"Was that long enough?" he asked. "I really don't think I can go on any longer with this bullshit."

I shook myself out of the trance he'd put me in and looked up from the camera.

"Perfect," Rodney said, walking toward Henry with a smile on his face. "You're going to make my life easy, man."

"Hmmm" was Henry's only response.

"Okay, let's call it a night. Tomorrow we need to get more B-roll of you walking around the city, eating at a restaurant, shit like that. Plus, I just heard from

Tyressa's crew, and they had a hell of time getting good footage today. So they need the extra time, too. We'll fly to Cancun on Thursday."

"Great," Henry said without enthusiasm. "So I have the night to myself?"

"Absolutely. You want me to get you a cab?" Rodney asked him.

Henry looked around him for a moment, then turned to me. "Are you guys taking the van back to the hotel?"

I nodded.

"Me and Chelsea have to take the equipment back and secure it. You want a ride?" Tom asked. I'd never felt so grateful in all my life. I looked at him like he'd just bought me a puppy.

Henry nodded.

"You coming?" Tom asked Rodney.

Rodney looked absolutely baffled for a moment. Then he seemed to shake it off. "Naw. Me and Ger will get a cab. Take off. Have a good night." He waved his hand in our direction dismissively.

Henry helped us pack up the equipment and then climbed into the van. I expected him to sit in the way back as he had during each ride so far. Instead, he opened the passenger side door for me, then climbed in right behind me. Tom, who was already in the driver's seat, made a double take but then shrugged and put the van in gear.

We rode in silence for a while. And I knew Tom was challenging me to speak to Henry. He gave me a quick sidelong glance several times. Henry stared out the window.

Finally, I took the challenge. "You really have a

way with words, Henry," I told him, shoving my glasses up on my nose, even though it was completely unnecessary.

"Thanks. I suppose it's helpful in my line of work. So I'll take that as encouragement that I don't have to quit my real job."

I shifted in my seat so I could see him better. "What is your real job?"

"I'm a writer. Freelance. And not very good at it, either."

"What makes you say that?" I asked.

"I'm here, right? If I could make a living as a writer, I wouldn't be here."

I scrunched up my brow. "Okay, don't get pissed. But from one rich kid to another, you can't be desperate."

Henry met my gaze, and for a split second I thought I'd pissed him off. But he gave me a small, crooked smile. "Well, Chelsea, as a rich kid with a day job, *you* must know I'm trying to make my own way."

I smiled. "Yeah. I get that."

"I tell you what," Tom said. "I'll let you both off the hook. You can just hand your trust funds over to me. Then I could retire right this minute."

"Tom's been trying to retire for years now," I explained. "The old man needs to get on with it, too, or he won't be able to walk well enough to spend his days golfing when he finally does."

"Whatever, kid. I'm still in good shape. It's Tim who can't keep up. We agreed to retire at the same time. And he's turned into a real whiny bastard lately. So I told him after this show I'd do it."

"Really?" I was shocked. We hadn't actually talked

about this, and deep down I'd selfishly hoped I would have Tom as my coworker until I was ready to leave Trek. "Oh, crap. I am going to miss you. Damn! Maybe this will be my last gig with Trek, too. I don't think I could put up with this shit without you."

"Tim's your partner?" Henry asked Tom.

"Yep. Thirty-two years."

"What does he do?"

"He's a dentist." Pride was easily discernible in Tom's voice

"See," I said, turning in my seat. "He whines about not having the money to retire, but Tim is a dentist. I mean, dentists do all right. We all know that. The real problem is Tom is afraid they'll get bored. No work, the kid is moved out of the house."

"Empty nest," Henry said knowingly. "My parents are going through that now my sister has graduated from college. She moved out for real and got her own place around the same time I moved to San Francisco. So now they're freaking out."

"When I left the house, my dad started painting," I told him, grinning. "He's terrible at it. My mom looked at his last attempt and told him to stick with being CEO."

My family owned a major real estate company in San Francisco. And, yeah, we were loaded. Everyone knew it, too, which is why Henry had heard of me when we first met. My brother Hayden was getting ready to take over as CEO, and my dad, who was supposed to have retired a couple years ago, was having trouble letting go. The hobby had been Hayden's idea because my dad was driving him crazy. So since the painting was a major fail, Hayden attempted to talk my dad into golf. My dad hated golf. I thought the whole thing was hilarious.

"My dad just recorded a new album," Henry said, laughing. "And my mom is volunteering at Channel Islands. They're cracking me up."

There was something so casual about this conversation in the van, it was easy to forget who I was talking to. It was easy to imagine he'd just said, "My dad has joined the local Elks club," rather than making a rock album that was no doubt going to go platinum within days of being released. In the darkened van, speeding along the highway, it was easy to imagine Henry as just another coworker out on a gig with us.

"Well, we're not quite empty nesters, yet," Tom said. "Brian works for Chelsea's brother, which means he doesn't make shit. So he's still at our place for now."

I laughed, but Henry looked confused. "Morrison and Sons seems like the kind of place that pays well," he said, a crease forming above his brow.

"It is," I told him. "But Tom's son works for my oldest brother, Jack, at his nonprofit."

"Right. I've read about this. Jack has a nonprofit that fights against real estate companies that evict people in order to gentrify their neighborhoods."

I nodded, smiling proudly. "That's right."

"That had to make for some interesting family conversation back when *your* family was making its living doing exactly that."

"You have no idea," I told him, shaking my head.

"But you all made it out of the family drama all right, I take it."

"We did. My brothers even managed not to kill each other. And I got a cool sister-in-law out of the deal."

Henry grinned. "You'll have to tell me that story someday."

"It requires a beer," Tom said.

"Over a beer, then," Henry agreed. His gaze held mine, and a smile lit up his perfect, handsome face.

Suddenly, the bubble popped, and I was unexpectedly nervous again. "Sure thing." I turned around in my seat to face forward.

Tom engaged Henry in a conversation about his dad's new album for the rest of the ride back to the hotel while I sat wringing my hands in my lap. How was I going to work with this man every day when one smile from him had me in knots?

Chapter 3

Seven months, two weeks, six days ago—New Orleans, Louisiana

Shooting B-roll was usually my least favorite part of the job. I'd worked with three different directors at Trek. All of them were overbearing and obnoxious, certain I required a massive amount of supervision and micromanagement. They were always demanding I shoot exactly what they wanted, not leaving any of it up to me. And what they wanted me to shoot was always stupid.

As a result, I never got to look around at my surroundings much. And I didn't get to truly practice my skills as a filmmaker. But Rodney was so checked out on this job, he couldn't care less. He let me shoot whatever I wanted as long as Henry was in the shot. It made my day.

Henry was happy, too, because Rodney didn't give a shit where we went in the city. He'd told Henry to choose. Henry had been to New Orleans before, and he took over driving the van. He showed us his favorite historic buildings, took us to eat at a killer Cajun restaurant, and followed the whole thing up with a walk in a park at sunset.

My crush got so much worse over the course of that day. Henry Rushton was cultured. He enjoyed art and architecture, was adventurous when it came to food, and appreciated the outdoors. He was everything I was attracted to.

When I'd actually kept a guy around for a while, all of those characteristics were requirements. I was pretty demanding of my boyfriends. The first two I'd had in college were more interested in playing video games than taking me out. And I figured out quickly I didn't need to put up with that shit. So I chose more carefully. I found out there were plenty of men who wanted to do the same things as me—watch old movies, go to museums and plays, walk in the woods. And I'd dated quite a few of them.

Tom liked to tease me about all the men I'd been through since I first discovered how much fun they could be six years ago. My mother and sister-in-law thought it was a healthy way of exploring what I wanted in a man. My brothers were always on edge, thinking I should date much less frequently than I did. And my dad would have preferred I was a nun.

But I was perfectly happy with how I conducted my love life. I wasn't indiscriminate. Far from it. I chose men carefully. They were clean, respectful, and I always had safe and satisfying sex. I just didn't keep them around very long. I tended to get bored easily. But I was okay with that, too.

The men I dated were not, however, *hot*. Not a one could make me drool on sight. But I'd never cared about that. It simply wasn't important. Eye candy didn't matter when compared to all the other elements of affection.

Henry Rushton, however, had the features of a man I'd love to date, *and* he was so smoking hot, I became physically warm just looking at him. So, from behind the safety of my camera, I crushed out on him. It was a strange interaction really. He spoke to me and Tom, occasionally Rodney, and rarely Gerry, as we went about our day. But I was always on the other side of the camera. It was like a curtain that kept me safely tucked away, a filter that defined our relationship. I was comfortable there, watching like a voyeur as Henry revealed himself in front of my eyes.

At the end of the day, we put the equipment away and climbed into the van. Just like it had been before, Gerry and Rodney took off after the shoot while Henry, Tom, and I headed back to the hotel. This time, Henry drove and Tom lounged in the back, while I perched nervously in the passenger seat.

"So, I heard a rumor once upon a time *you* were supposed to be the CEO of Morrison and Sons, not your brother Hayden," Henry said casually.

"Once upon a time, that was something my dad had in mind, yeah," I answered honestly.

"So…what happened?"

"I insisted he change the name from Morrison and Sons to Morrison and People." I shrugged. "Turns out it was a deal breaker."

A chuckle rose from Tom in the back seat.

Henry smiled. "Okay, you don't want to answer that. I get it. Different question. How did you get into *this*?"

"I want to make movies. I went to film school and got this gig afterward. It's a good start."

"Ha!" Tom said. "She could have had an even better start, but she wouldn't take the other jobs offered to her."

I turned in my seat and shot Tom a dirty look. My disinterest in taking a job offered to me only because of my last name was not something I wanted to discuss.

"Been there," Henry said knowingly. "Do you like working for Trek?"

"I like the work. I think I'm good at it. But this will probably be my last gig with Trek. Especially since this jackass is going to retire," I said, pointing my thumb toward Tom.

"Eight months." Henry sighed. "It feels like a long time."

I laughed. "Over it already?"

"I don't know. I *am* looking forward to going to some of the locations."

"Yeah, like where?" Tom asked.

"Well, I've been to all the spots we're heading to in the US. But I haven't been to very many places overseas."

"Wait." I turned in my seat to face him. "You've been to *all* the shoot locations in the US?"

"I'm well traveled," he said with a grin. "At least in the country. We went on a lot of family trips. And I went on a couple of tours with my dad."

"I guess that makes sense," I conceded. His dad was a damn rock star. It was easy to forget when I was busy ogling him all the time.

"But my dad is afraid of heights."

"Really?"

"Yeah. Very, very afraid of heights. So he hates to fly. I've only been overseas a couple of times. I went once on break in college with some friends, and once last year with my cousin. But I have a lot more ground I'd like to cover. This show will at least be a chance to do that."

"The travel is my favorite part of the job, too." Well, that and filming Henry all day.

"What's next, anyway?" Henry asked.

"Cancun, followed by Vegas."

"Great. They'll probably have me stuck in bars and nightclubs every night," he said in exasperation.

I laughed. "You suck at the playboy thing, you know. My brother Hayden excelled at it. You should take lessons."

"No, thanks. I'll stick with being 'boring Henry.' "

"Boring?"

"That's what Tyressa calls me. In fact, I'm surprised she didn't talk Ken and Steve out of casting me in this show. She's been convinced I'm the most boring person on the planet since she was fourteen and I was sixteen and she tried to persuade me to smoke a joint in the bathroom during a party at my aunt's house."

"And you didn't?"

"No. And I stole the joint from her and flushed it down the toilet."

"Damn. You're a Boy Scout," Tom said.

"No. I was too busy with sports to do Boy Scouts."

I laughed. "What kind of rocker's kid are you?"

Henry glanced at me for a brief moment before turning back to the road. A rakish grin played on his face. "Not a very good one, I guess. My cousin Danny is much better at it, though. He's the one who should be on this show. He'd love going to bars and clubs, and he'd love the attention of the cameras." Henry bit the right side of his bottom lip for a second. "Maybe I'll have him meet up with us somewhere. That would make for a good show."

"I'm sure Steve would be all over that," Tom said. "He's already mentioned trying to get as many of your family members on the show as possible.

Henry rolled his eyes. "Well, Danny won't be an issue. He'll do it if he has the time."

"What does he do?" I asked.

"He just started a music studio with my uncle. But it's *his* thing. Uncle Hank is fronting the money but staying out of the business. Danny is smart about music, and he's great with people, but he doesn't know shit about managing a business so he's up to his eyeballs at the moment."

Henry pulled into our hotel parking lot, and I was sorry the conversation was coming to an end. The van ride home was becoming my favorite part of the day.

"Your family is fascinating," Tom said.

Henry laughed. "Not really. They are probably more boring than you'd expect. I'll tell you about them sometime." He pulled the van into a spot at the far end of the lot and turned it off.

"How about now?" I asked, unwilling to let him go just yet. "Over a beer?" I suggested, pushing my glasses up.

Henry turned in his seat to look at me more fully. "Deal. If you'll tell me why Chelsea Morrison gave up an empire to be my camerawoman."

"You two have fun," Tom said, sliding open the van door. "I gotta call my hubby and my kid. And don't forget, we have an early flight in the morning."

****

Henry and I had just settled in at the hotel bar, each with a glass of red wine in our hands, when they came in. Tyressa breezed into the room like a movie star walking the red carpet. She was followed by two of her friends. They'd flown in earlier in the day to visit with her. They were even louder now and wearing even less clothing.

I could see Henry shrinking in his chair as if he could somehow hide all six feet and four inches of himself. It didn't work, of course. Tyressa and her entourage walked up to us. Before we could do anything about it, they pulled extra chairs from nearby tables and squeezed in around us.

I moved instinctively to push my chair up against Henry's so none of the girls could pry their way between us. Henry smiled at me gratefully. Neither Henry nor I spoke for a good ten minutes as the three women descended upon us and chattered inanely.

"Henry! I told the girls you'd be here!" Tyressa squealed. She leaned around me toward Henry, practically shoving her shoulder into my neck and burying me in a cloud of perfume.

Henry's lack of a response did nothing to discourage their focus on him. And all three women fawned over him as if he were a puppy dog in the store window. I was trying to figure out an extraction plan when I saw a man and woman walk into the bar across the room. The man had a large camera around his neck. The woman held a tablet in her hands as her head swiveled from side to side, scanning the room.

I knew paparazzi when I saw them, so I shouted over the din of excited airheads. "Hey! I think the press is here."

Mouths snapped shut and heads pivoted as all three women turned to follow the direction of my pointing finger. It was exactly the distraction we needed. Before the girls even had a chance to start waving frantically at the reporter, Henry grabbed my hand and pulled. I tumbled out of the chair and followed him.

Chapter 4

Henry moved quickly, tugging me along behind him. In a half crouch, we jogged away from the front of the bar. After weaving through the haphazardly arranged tables, we burst through a set of metal swinging doors and into the kitchen.

The staff all paused in midmotion to stare at us. Henry stood to his full height and gave the whole lot of them a sexy, crooked grin. Despite the fact that four out of five of them were men, it worked.

The massive man behind the grill chuckled and pointed to another door to our left. Henry nodded, and I waved as he pulled me toward the door. When we went through it, we were in the far corner of the bar. We could be seen clearly by the bartender but were mostly hidden from everyone else.

The bartender was a short, built, absolutely gorgeous man with a trim beard and hair halfway to his shoulders. He walked over to us right away. His gaze paused on Henry for a moment before turning to me. He winked at me, then looked back at Henry.

"You're Henry Rush, aren't you?" he asked.

Instead of being irritated by this, like I though he would, Henry grinned. "Yeah. My dad's Sean." It was the first time I'd heard him acknowledge it proudly rather than shrink from the fame by association.

"Love his music, man," the bartender said.

"Me, too," Henry replied.

"What can I get for you and gorgeous here?" he asked, gesturing in my direction with his head.

Henry looked at me, amused grin still firmly in place. "What do you want, gorgeous?"

I bit my lip and pretended to deliberate. I hadn't felt so desirable in…maybe ever. With two hot men watching me, I pushed my glasses up and grabbed a wine list. I perused it slowly. Neither man moved. When someone on the other end of the bar called out to the bartender in front of me, he waved his hand and told them to cool their jets.

Finally, I selected a bottle of wine. Henry held up two fingers. The bartender nodded and produced both bottles along with two glasses. I grabbed the glasses while Henry took the bottles, and we went back into the kitchen. This time the big man behind the grill pointed to another door at the back of the kitchen. It led out into the hallway of the hotel, and we made our way from there to the elevator and up to Henry's suite.

I was laughing hard as Henry shut the door behind us. "I guess what they say is true. You really do hate the spotlight. I've never seen someone run away from the press so fast in my life."

He grinned and nodded. "I always have." Henry set the glasses on the small round table and settled into a chair on one side of it. "But who says I was running from the press? I was mostly running from Tyressa and her minions." He looked at one of the bottles, hefting it in his hands. "Good choice by the way."

I plopped into the chair on the opposite side of the table. "Are you a connoisseur or something?"

Henry looked up at me. He looked like the ultimate

bad boy. He could easily have graced the cover of a novel about the leader of a motorcycle gang that steals the heart of a young, innocent girl. His long, midnight black hair was loose right then, having been let out of its tidy ponytail down in the bar. His sharp nose and dark eyes were penetrating as he sat back and said, "I've always liked wine best. I come from a long line of beer people, and don't get me wrong, I like beer—good beer, that is—but a fine red wine, that's always been my favorite."

"You are a contradiction, Henry Rushton."

He shrugged. "Only if you believe in stereotypes." He tugged the wrapper off the wine easily. "Oh shit! We need a corkscrew."

I stood and walked over to the kitchenette. "A fancy-ass suite like this, there has to be one in here somewhere." I pulled open the drawer beneath the microwave and held up the object in question. "Ah ha! See."

"Stayed in a lot of fancy-ass hotels, Chels?"

I'd been walking back toward the table when he'd said it. The nickname was what had me stopping me in my tracks. I stared at Henry, my brain on pause.

He held out his hand for the corkscrew. Then he, too, paused and cocked his head at me. "What? Am I not supposed to call you Chels?"

"I'm not sure," I told him, finally moving again. I handed him the corkscrew and sat back down in my chair. "You probably heard Tom call me that."

Henry nodded as he worked the top of the wine bottle.

"Other than Tom, the only people in the world who call me that are my brothers and my dad. In fact, my brother Jack kind of started calling me that when we were kids, and I hated it."

"And now?" he asked, pulling the glasses toward him to pour the wine.

"Now, I don't hate it. And it's reserved for certain people."

"Ah. An affectionate nickname. I get it. Enough said, Chelsea." He slid a full glass of wine over to me and held his own up. I clinked his glass and took a sip.

"Not bad. Even though you didn't let it breathe."

"I'm not that fancy. I wanted it in my belly." Henry settled back in his chair. "We have kind of a nickname thing in my family, too."

"Yeah?" I leaned toward him, my arms resting on the table. "You were going to tell me about your family."

Henry smiled. "It's a little convoluted."

"Mine's boring and straightforward. Mom, dad, two brothers, one sister-in-law, and one bachelor uncle. We have a family business. Blah, blah, blah. Let me live vicariously. Lay it on me."

"So my dad was just this ordinary kid from Michigan. And he got into music young, you know? He was just starting out when he met Hank, and they became best friends. Hank was kind of a mentor to my dad. Anyway, they started helping each other with albums and touring together. Hank was already pretty famous, and my dad would open for him. Then later, when my dad got famous, Hank would open for him. They've been doing it that way for forty years."

"And how did your dad meet your mom? I mean, she was a park ranger, right? How does a park ranger meet a rock star? Was she a groupie?"

He laughed. "No, nothing ordinary like that. They picked her up hitchhiking. Anyway, they met and fell in love, and that's where I came in. They were so tight with Hank, they named me after him, because of course, his real name is Henry."

"And you have a sister, Gloria?"

He nodded. "She's named after my grandmother."

"Is Hank's kid named after anyone?"

"Yeah, my dad. His real name is Sean Daniel. But my uncle is kind of the king of nicknames. So he called him 'Danny' from birth, and it stuck. He calls my mom 'Baby,' and that really stuck. I don't think most people even know her real name."

"What about you, do you have a nickname?" I asked.

"Hmmm." He shifted uncomfortably in his chair. "I don't have one, at least not a nickname that *everyone* calls me."

I could sense he was hiding something. "You're stalling," I accused.

Henry let out a deep sigh. "My dad calls me 'Buddy.' It started when I was a little bitty kid, but he still does it to this very day. It's embarrassing as hell. But who's gonna argue with my dad?" He shrugged.

"Buddy?"

"Don't dwell, or I'll call you Chels," he threatened.

I still wasn't sure I would mind. But I ignored that and asked him, "Who are you closest to?"

"Damn. That's a hard question."

"I can tell you I love all my family. But to be honest, I'm closest to my oldest brother, Jack. No denying it."

"If I had to pick…I guess I'd have to say my dad."

He shrugged. "But that's just because we are a lot alike."

"Hmmm." I decided to rib him until I got the information I really wanted. "But he wouldn't ever do anything like this?"

"You mean the show? No, he wouldn't. In fact, I'm still reeling from the fact that *I* got talked into it."

"So, how did that happen?"

Henry filled my glass back up. "No way. I just told you my convoluted family tree. It's your turn. I want to know how *you* ended up here."

It was getting easier to talk to Henry by the minute. He had a quiet, calming presence, and I was feeling relaxed. So I sat back in my chair, propping my feet on the rungs of the table and rested my wine glass in my hands. "When I was in seventh grade, my oldest brother, Jack, took off."

"Took off?"

"Yep. He disappeared. Went to Rio, it turned out. He called every few months so we knew he was alive, but that was it. No visits, nothing. He was gone for five long years."

"That must have been hard, especially since you're close."

"It was," I admitted. "He wrote me letters regularly. But it wasn't the same. Jack's leaving was really hard on me." I shifted in my seat. "Anyway, when he came back, he made it crystal clear he was no longer the heir apparent to run the company. In fact, as you know, he set up his nonprofit to fight the company and everything it did."

"How did that go over?" Henry asked, a very sincere look of interest on his gorgeous face.

"Better than you would expect. My parents were happy to have Jack back. And my dad couldn't argue that the family business wasn't bad for people. So he let Jack do his thing, and he set changes in motion that would eventually lead to a whole different kind of company. But the bottom line was he still needed someone to leave the helm to. My uncle never had any kids, so that left me and Hayden."

"And you already said Hayden was a playboy," he pointed out.

"Like you wouldn't believe. He was straight out of a TV exposé. He partied, he hung out on yachts, and narrowly escaped prosecution in far-off countries. And he dated girls like…"

"Tyressa?"

I laughed. "Exactly like her. Meanwhile, I was studying my ass off and getting good grades. Valedictorian at my prep school," I told him proudly.

"I have no doubt."

"So, my dad decided I was the one who would lead the company one day."

"Only you had other ideas?"

"I sure did. I'd been in charge of making the family movies since I was about five. And then I was making them for friends. And I was in the film club at school. And when Jack came back, I made documentaries for him about the housing problem. It was my passion. I wanted to make movies. I wanted to be the next Ken Burns. So I went to a school that had both a film major and a business school. With my dad satisfied that I was going to school to be the next CEO of Morrison and Sons, I took the classes *I* wanted to take."

"Right under his nose," Henry said, raising his

glass to me.

"For a while. But I eventually told him."

"And?" he coaxed.

"He was pissed. And he was understanding, disappointed, and loving all at once. He's kind of confusing like that."

"Hmmm," Henry mumbled knowingly.

"Did your dad want you to be a musician?" I asked.

"No. But we're not on me yet. So, you went to film school. What happened next?"

"I took an unpaid internship that I absolutely loved. Then when I graduated, I got some suspicious job offers."

"Suspicious?"

"Yeah, friends or business acquaintances of my dad's were calling, offering me jobs I wasn't anywhere near qualified for. So I turned them all down and took a job with Trek. It pays crap, they treat me like I'm an imbecile, even though I'm the best they have, and people apologize when I tell them where I work. But this is the path I'm taking. No shortcuts."

"Good for you," Henry said, raising his glass to me before finishing his wine.

I finished my own wine and set the glass back on the table. "And now it's your turn."

He stood. "How about we do it over margaritas in Cancun? I gotta get some sleep before getting stuck on a tiny jet with Tyressa for several hours tomorrow."

The travel situation had us all on the same chartered plane. But, as small as it was, the thing was still separated into classes. Snarky Steve insisted Henry sit up front with him, Tyressa, and the two directors, Rodney and Heath. That left me, Tom, and Gerry in the back with the other crew. I didn't care. I sat with Tom and bullshitted or slept through the flights. But, apparently, it was a little rougher for Henry.

I stood and made my way to the door. "I'm going to hold you to that."

"Don't worry. I won't go back on my word. I enjoy talking to you, Chelsea."

My stomach wanted to grow butterflies, or flip over, or quiver. But I didn't let it. Henry was a coworker I could talk to just like Tom. Okay, maybe not like Tom. But I wasn't going to let my stupid crush on a man I could never have ruin a pleasant companionship on this hell trip.

Chapter 5

Seven   months,   two   weeks   ago—Jackson,
Mississippi

Tom threw his equipment bag in the back of the van and slammed the door closed before stalking to the driver's side and practically assaulting the seat with his ass. Henry and I, both already in the van, watched him before turning to exchange a glance of confusion.

Tom wrenched the key in the ignition and reached to shift gears. I put my hand over his, stopping him. "Hey, Tom. Is everything okay?"

Tom moved his hand off the gearshift and sat back in the seat. "Oh, Chels," he said, a deep sigh leaving his lips.

I was really starting to worry. I looked over my shoulder at Henry, who was perched in the back seat, leaning forward. His brow was furrowed. I turned back to Tom. "What's going on, Tom?"

Tom turned to look at me. "I had a drink with that Jake kid last night," he said, referring to the cameraman on Tyressa's crew. "You know this is that little punk's first gig with Trek?"

"Yeah. So?"

"Fuck, Chels. He's a newbie. Fresh out of college. He doesn't have your experience, and he isn't half as good as you. They throw out at least a third of the shit he films."

"And?" I asked again.

"And he makes more money than you! He showed me his fucking pay stub."

I went still. I wasn't sure how the hell I was supposed to react to that.

"Maybe they just forgot to give you a raise you were supposed to get," Henry suggested gently.

I ran a hand down the side of my face and answered automatically, truthfully. "No, I just got a raise at the beginning of this gig."

"So. What happened? The kid was a tough negotiator?" Henry had a strange tone in his voice. It sounded a lot like desperation.

"The little fucker said that he didn't negotiate at all. They just offered it to him," Tom growled. "Believe me, I asked for the fucking details."

"Shit," Henry whispered.

My stomach hurt. "Look, let's just go. We're supposed to meet Steve in a few minutes."

"Fuck Steve!" Tom said. "This is his fault. He's in charge of personnel on this show. He picked those fucking salary rates."

I leaned back in my seat and folded my arms across my chest. "There's nothing we can do about it, Tom. There's no need to get worked up about it."

Both men stared at me, mouths dropped open.

"Chelsea, don't you see what's happening here?" Tom said. "You are being paid less because you have tits! This is bullshit!"

"Total bullshit," Henry echoed.

"Look, *I'm* the one with the tits. *I'm* the one who should be worked up here. And I'm not. Just drive."

But it was a lie. I was practically shaking.

"Fuck," Tom grumbled, putting the van into gear and pulling out into traffic.

****

Seven months ago—Miami, Florida

I hadn't done anything about the equal pay situation. Tom had dropped the subject. As for Henry, even if he'd wanted to bring it up, he wouldn't have had a chance. Outside of looking at him through the viewfinder of my camera, I'd barely seen him at all since New Orleans because when we weren't shooting, Rodney had me and Tom sitting in a dark room with him cutting film every night.

I'd also never gotten that promised margarita with Henry, meaning that I still hadn't satisfied my curiosity about why he was even doing all this. Meanwhile, Henry and Tyressa limped from town to town trying to make their assignments appear to be even remotely interesting to them. From Cancun to Vegas to Dallas, Steve sent Henry to bars, clubs, and strip joints while Tyressa snoozed her way through plays, museums, and upscale restaurants.

I watched as Steve got crankier and crankier. Then, finally, in Miami, he seemed to completely lose his shit. He snapped at everyone on the plane all the way there. Then he demanded as soon as we hit the hotel everyone should drop their stuff in their rooms and meet him in the conference room off the lobby.

He was pacing at one end of the room, a scowl on his face, as we all shuffled in. Steve didn't bother to look at any of us until we were all seated around the oval table. I exchanged a glance with Tom, who just shook his head.

Steve spun around. "We have a problem. I just got off the phone with Ken. He showed the first episode of the show to a test audience." He paused for dramatic effect. "And they hated it."

Gerry slumped over. Tyressa's crew all dropped their jaws as if this was somehow shocking. I wasn't shocked, and neither was Tom. I looked over at Henry. And he looked...almost pleased.

"Why?" Tyressa cried.

"They loved you," Steve told her. "And Henry. In fact, the ratings for the two of you were through the roof. The men think you're hot, and the women are crazy for Henry."

Henry rolled his eyes, and I suppressed a laugh.

"Then what's the problem?" Jake asked. I glared at his more-money-making ass.

Steve answered the question but directed it at Henry and Tyressa. "Apparently, they don't think you look like you're having fun. In fact, the audience overwhelming agreed you both looked like you were in pain."

"That's because you're sending them to the wrong places." Every eye in the room turned to me after my outburst, and I could feel myself shrinking into the chair. I pushed my glasses up on my nose and tried to look confident.

"The audience didn't seem to have any problem with the locations," Steve snapped in his snarkiest voice.

"That's not what she means." Henry turned away from me to look at Steve. His voice, usually quiet and smooth, was raised and rough. "You're sending Tyressa to museums and shows when she would much rather be out shopping or partying at clubs."

"I would," Tyressa said, nodding her head vigorously.

"With all due respect, someone has to do the cultural side of these cities, Henry," Steve argued.

"Let me do it. I couldn't care less about all these places you've been sending me to. I'd be more than happy to do the cultural sites," Henry argued.

There was a deep silence in the room. Steve started pacing again, his hands clasped behind his back, his head down. We all watched him. After a good three or four minutes of this little demonstration, Steve stopped and looked up at us all. "Look, Ken is determined to make this show work. And we have to come up with something. So let's put our heads together."

"Are you serious?" Tom said, exasperated. "Henry just came up with your solution."

"Whatever. Let's just cancel the damn thing instead," Henry said, folding his arms over his chest, signaling that he was completely done with this asinine conversation.

I knew Henry hated this job, but I didn't want him to give up. Because even though I hadn't exactly been on cloud nine over the past month, I wasn't willing to give up the time with my crush. Also, I hadn't applied for any other jobs. I could use the next seven months to prepare for my next move.

Steve looked over at Henry, then addressed Tom. "Henry's idea—that's not an option."

"Why not! What's wrong with Henry's idea?" Tyressa asked, a pout forming on her lips. "I would *love* to go to the bars and clubs."

Steve let out a huge sigh and plopped into the chair

at the head of the table. "Because what we *do* have going for us is that women dig Henry. They're not going to want to watch a hot, young dude go to museums and shit."

"I completely disagree." My mouth was getting me into serious trouble, and once again all eyes in the room turned to me. I squirmed in my seat as they all examined me. I kept my gaze on Steve, purposefully not looking at Henry.

"Chelsea is right. Most of the women I know would say a cultured man is sexy." I was shocked by the amused lilt Henry's voice had suddenly taken on.

"Well, Tyressa, as the only other woman in the room, do you agree?"

"Um...I guess," she said.

"I think a cultured man is sexy," Tom interjected. "Don't I count?"

"Sure...I guess. But you have to admit that you are smaller portion of the population," Steve said, clearly uncomfortable.

Henry chuckled, and I turned to him. He winked at Tom and then addressed Steve again. "Why don't we just try it? At this point, we don't have anything to lose."

Steve seemed to be deep in thought as he examined Henry closely. He rubbed his chin and stared. Finally, he nodded. "Sure. What the hell?"

****

Six months and two weeks ago—Washington, DC

A temperate breeze wafted in through the window, and I took a deep breath. Another day was over. The beautiful weather, glory of springtime in the city, and the presence of Henry Rushton made me warm all over.

"To Chelsea, who's a freaking genius," Henry said, raising his glass.

I blushed as I raised my own glass to clink it with his and Tom's. Then I took a long gulp. After two weeks of a grueling schedule, we'd managed to wrap up a new episode and ship it off to Ken. Tonight, we'd gotten word the new episode had been a hit with test audiences.

"It wasn't all me," I said meekly.

"Bullshit. You saved the show," Henry said. "*And* you should be getting a raise for it." I rolled my eyes. Henry gave me a stern look. "To be continued."

I still hadn't done anything about my equal pay situation. At least, not anything concrete. I had, in fact, been reading up on job fairness and gender inequalities in pay, particularly in traditionally male-oriented careers like mine. I had also talked to Candace about the whole thing, and we'd discussed what my legal options were if I was unable to negotiate with my boss. I was formulating a solid plan before moving forward. But I hadn't shared any of that with Henry or Tom.

"I guess this means I'm stuck with this gig for a few more months," Tom grumbled.

Grateful for the change in subject, I elbowed him and smiled. "You're just cranky because you need to get laid. When's Tim coming to meet up with us, anyway?"

"In New York. Just four more days."

"Way to make me jealous, man. I don't have a silver lining. We saved the show, now I have to finish the damn thing." Henry grinned. "And I don't even have someone flying in every couple weeks to keep me company."

I leaned back in the chair I was sitting in, wishing that the thing could completely hide me away as my thoughts wandered to all the ways I could keep Henry company.

Tom sat in a chair opposite mine, and Henry sat on the couch between us in the spacious living area of his hotel suite. The three of us had escaped up there as soon as the meeting was over. We'd brought up a bottle of wine and one of those cheese and sausage baskets that was presented to us as a gift from the hotel for shooting at their place. And now we were decompressing after having learned it looked like the show was going to make it after all.

Henry put his feet his up on the coffee table in front of him and crossed his ankles. "Well, it's a little more fun now, anyway. Tomorrow, we hit the Air and Space Museum. I always liked that place. I've been there a few times, so I already know all the best places to go for the show."

Henry had essentially taken over as writer and director for his segments. He decided where we went, what we filmed, and what he said on camera. It made for great television. And, Steve, recognizing that, had sent Rodney and Gerry to work with Tyressa, having fired her director. So Tom, Henry, and I spent our days running around the cities, and as of a few nights ago, Henry joined Tom and me in the editing room as well.

"How many times have you been to that museum?" Tom asked.

"Every time I'm in DC. I always hit that one. And if I was with my mom, which was most of the time, we always had to go to the Natural History Museum. My sister, the artist, has to choose more carefully because there are so many art museums."

"So your entire family is full of museum geeks?" I asked.

Henry smiled and nodded. "My immediate family, anyway."

"What about your dad?" I had to ask.

Henry's dad stood six foot six inches tall, as wide as a refrigerator, covered from head to toe in tattoos, and was a hard-rock star. But Henry always talked about him like he was the normal guy who lived next door on any average American suburban street. It fascinated me, and I wasn't the only one who was curious about Sean Rush. Tom leaned forward perceptibly in his chair when I asked.

Henry shrugged. "He likes museums. Mostly, though, he likes watching us enjoy museums." For a second, I thought that was all he would say on the subject. But then he looked at me and Tom and seemed to grasp that we wanted more. And he gave it to us. "My dad enjoys exactly two things in life." He held up a finger. "Music." He held up a second finger. "And making the people he loves happy. And not necessarily in that order. He married a park ranger who loves museums, historic sites, and parks. They had a daughter who's an artist and a son who's a writer. And we're all major museum geeks," he said, looking at me as he used my words again. "So, if we are, he is."

Tom leaned back in his chair. "Rarely do you meet someone with such a vast chasm between his personal life and his public persona."

Henry shrugged. "Everyone who knows him is always so baffled by it. But I don't think it's so strange. And believe me, there are more like him out there."

"Families are kind of an envelope," I said.

"Envelope?" Henry asked me.

"Yeah, if you look inside an envelope, without pulling out the contents, you can only see a portion of the items or maybe even a distorted view of them. But everything looks completely different if you take them out and unfold them." Tom and Henry both stared at me. "Okay, so I'm not a writer like you; I'm a filmmaker, and it makes sense from my perspective. It's all about viewpoint. Take my father for example."

"Yeah, see, now, I find *him* to be pretty fascinating," Henry said.

"Why? What does he look like when you peer into the envelope?"

"Well, he's this rich, successful businessman, right? And he made his way in the world by expanding his father's company. And it was the kind of business where you had to be ruthless and cutthroat. I mean, your dad threw people out of their homes and built high-end condos on the property." Henry almost looked apologetic after saying this, and he paused.

"True," I said, nodding. "Continue."

"So then, his oldest son, the one who is supposed to inherit the company, turns against him and starts a nonprofit to fight his own father. And after years of this fighting, the company does a one-eighty and starts to develop low income housing and specializes in historic renovations."

"Yep. So? What does that look like?"

"No idea. That's just it. It doesn't make sense."

"Exactly," I said. "Because you weren't in my house when my brother, Jack, left for five years. You didn't see the toll that took on my father. You weren't in my house when Jack came back. You didn't see the relief on my dad's face. You weren't there when they sat down together, at least once a week, and had a meal and a conversation. You didn't see the way Jack talked passionately about what the company could be if it changed. And you didn't see the pride in my father's eyes when he did it. So, you can't have the same perspective as me. Just like I can't have the same perspective on your father as you do. He just looks scary to me."

Henry laughed. "He is far from scary."

"Tell that to my fight or flight instinct," Tom quipped. "Because I'm pretty sure I'd go *way* out of my way to never make *this dude* mad." Tom pulled up a picture of Sean Rush on his phone, and he held it out to us.

I could see his point. In the image, which was probably about twenty years old, Sean wore a black tank top that showcased a set of massive biceps covered in ink. His black hair hung loose and wild around his shoulders. His dark brown eyes looked feral beneath mashed-together eyebrows that spoke of anger and vengeance.

Henry laughed harder and wiped at his eyes, then he turned to me, still looking amused. "What about me? Do you think *I'm* scary?"

"No," I said automatically.

"No?" He frowned a big fake frown. "But I look a lot like my dad. Everyone says so. And I'm not that much smaller."

"Hmmm. No tattoos," I said.

"Not true." Henry pulled his feet off the table and jumped up. He took two steps until he stood right in front of me. My breath hitched in my throat as he took his shirt off in one clean motion. "See?"

Chapter 6

I could not breathe. I could not think. I was pretty sure my heart was beating, but I couldn't spare a moment to check. Henry Rushton stood in front of me, bare-chested, and he was perhaps the most beautiful thing I'd ever seen.

His chest was only slightly paler than his deeply tanned arms. His muscles were sculpted and hard, but not so big as to be intimidating. He had this tiny little patch of dark black hair right in the center of his chest, between two perfect, round nipples. I wanted to lick them.

"Two here." He pointed to the tattoos just below his collarbone on either side of his chest. I blinked my eyes and tried to focus on them. One was a pen and paper, while the other appeared to be sheet of music. "And one here." He turned around to reveal a smooth and perfectly massage-able back with one long tattoo stretching across his shoulder blades. I didn't recognize the design. I might have categorized it as tribal, but it looked more ancient than any I'd ever seen.

My fingers twitched to reach up and touch him, but I managed to keep my hands to myself long enough for Henry to put his shirt back on and sit down on the couch again. "Does that count?" he asked with a grin, his eyes locked on me.

I shrugged and pulled my gaze away from him to

glance over at Tom, whose mouth flopped open like a fish as he stared at Henry. "I don't know. It's only three. Your dad has like a million. What do you think, Tom?" I asked as I reached up with my forefinger and pushed on the bridge of my glasses.

Tom managed to close his mouth and he cleared his throat. "Not scary, no."

"Damn. Well, I tried." Henry took a sip of his wine and then laughed like he'd thought of a joke.

"What?" I asked.

"My dad's tattoos. They're not skulls and shit, you know. They're like archaeological finds, animals, and names. He has my mom's and mine and my sister's names. It's all stuff like that. Pretty tame, really."

"Okay, I get it. He's a teddy bear."

He laughed and nodded. "That's about right."

"And so are you," I told him.

Henry looked at me for a long moment, a smile curving his lips. "I suppose you have my number, Chels." He paused and a crease formed between his eyebrows. "Sorry, Chelsea."

"Okay," Tom said, standing up. "It's past this old man's bedtime. We have to get up early and follow you all over the city with cameras. So, I'm going to hit the hay."

An internal war ensued inside my brain at that moment. I wanted to stay right where I was. But I'd seen enough of the forbidden fruit for one night. And if Henry and I were left alone, things might only get awkward. I didn't need that. So I pulled myself up and followed Tom out of the room, wishing Henry a good night on my way.

****

Six months, one week, and two days ago—New York, New York

"You would think you could at least *pretend* to like me, Henry! I mean, Jesus, I'm *trying* here! I'm being a professional!" Tyressa screamed.

Henry did what he'd been doing for the last five minutes, sitting across from her at an elaborately set table, arms folded over his chest, eyes staring off into the distance, exasperated expression just barely suppressed on his face. He hadn't said a single word since she'd started yelling at him.

Neither had anyone else for that matter. In fact, the entire restaurant was quiet. Luckily, we'd rented the place out for the day and there were no patrons in there, just staff, with mouths held open and camera phones pointed discreetly in their direction.

Tyressa must have finally gotten tired of the silent treatment, because she asked him, "Well, don't you have anything to say for yourself?"

Henry leaned forward, placing his forearms on the table. "Look, Tyressa," he said in a low, calm voice. "We just got here. It's only our second night in New York. I know both you and I would probably like some time to explore the city a little, shoot our individual scenes, before we do this joint scene. That would be easier, wouldn't it?"

She seemed to be stunned into silence, so she just nodded.

"So, why don't you let me talk to Steve for a minute and maybe we can do this in a few days. It would make the scene so much better, don't you think?"

"But, Henry," she said, her voice much softer.

"The issue is you are supposed to look like you *want* me. And Henry, everyone wants me." Her voice started to rise. "Everyone but you!"

"Tyressa," Henry said quietly, reaching out to catch her hand in his. "That's not the issue. The issue is we're just not ready to do this scene yet. We should do this on Thursday instead."

She stared at him for a long moment, then nodded slowly.

"Steve," Henry said, leaning back in his chair and letting go of Tyressa's hand. "Can we rebook?"

"Aww fuck," Steve said. "We already paid for this place, Henry."

"Don't worry about it," the restaurant's owner said, stepping forward. "We can make it happen." She'd been watching the entire scene with the same rapt attention as the rest of us, and she had a mixture of shock and admiration on her face.

"Fine. Then let's get out of here and let them open up," Steve grumbled.

I packed up my equipment quickly. Everyone else was much faster at packing up than me. So I wasn't surprised when Henry ended up beside me, hefting one of my bags. "Now that I got us out of that, where would you like to go tonight, Chelsea?"

I wasn't looking at him at that moment. And maybe that helped. Because I answered as if Tom had asked me. "I want ice cream."

"Ice cream," Henry repeated.

I stood and shoved the last bag over my shoulder. "Yep."

He flashed a killer smile. "I happen to know a place."

"I bet you do."

Henry moved to the door and held it open for me. "My aunt used to live here, you know. And she showed me all the best local spots."

"Lead the way."

****

Henry and I were alone at the café. Well, we weren't really alone. There were at least a dozen other patrons in there, but none of the other crew from the show. Tom, who was the only one who shared our rental car with us these days, had chosen to get a cab back to the hotel where Tim waited for him. And we hadn't bothered to invite anyone else.

"All right, Rushton. It's time to spill," I said, pulling a massive scoop of fudgy ice cream out of the bottom of my glass dish. "Why are you doing this show?"

Henry settled back in the booth and looked at me with amusement. "It's been killing you, hasn't it?"

"More and more every day. I could tell from the beginning you weren't into this assignment. But it's become increasingly clear you were probably dragged into it kicking and screaming."

Henry smiled at me, and as it always did, my stomach quivered. "Well, I don't know. It's better than I expected it to be now that I get to do whatever I want and go wherever I want."

"But there's still Tyressa," I said with a wink.

"Ugh. Yes. You know, when I found out she was involved, I almost backed out again."

"Tell the story, Henry," I urged.

He ignored my plea and continued to talk about Tyressa. "I called my aunt last night to ask her how to pull this off."

"Pull it off?"

"Yeah. I'm supposed to look at her like she's—"

"Interesting, engaging, and sexy." I repeated Steve's words.

"Exactly. I'm a writer, not an academy-award-winning actor."

I laughed. "What did your aunt say?"

"She wished me luck. She's known Tyressa since she was a baby."

"I bet it was a blast working with her dad all those years," I said with a touch of sarcasm.

"Actually, Roger wasn't too bad. Aunt Stacey told me they were like a family. It's pretty great when you have a work family." He looked up at me. "Like me, you, and Tom."

An intense feeling of warmth spread through my entire being just then. And I couldn't speak, so I just nodded.

"All right." He completely abandoned his ice cream and folded his arms across his chest. "I'll tell you why I took this gig. I was dead broke."

"Dead broke with a trust fund?" I raised my eyebrow.

"A trust fund I didn't want to touch. Just like you, my friend, I tried to make it on my own. Only it was damn hard to do as a freelance writer."

"Using a pen name," I pointed out.

He sighed. "Yes. Because if I sent in a story with my real name on it, I would never know if it got published because it was good or because of my name. So, just like you won't take a better job that you acquired because of your family name, neither will I."

"Yeah, I get it. So you were broke and in San Francisco?"

"Yes. I moved up there after college. I wanted to have some distance between my family and me so I could make it on my own. But..." He ran his hand over his ponytailed hair.

"Not too much distance," I prompted.

"It's embarrassing as hell to admit, but, no. I didn't want to go too far away. But I needed a new town at least, you know?"

I nodded, encouraging him to continue.

"But I wasn't making it."

"SF is stupid expensive," I said knowingly.

"Tell me about it. I ended up having to move in with my mom's brother, Uncle Brad."

"Desperate for a day job?"

"Yes. But I planned to take a job at a library or something. Then I got the call from Ken."

"How did he talk you into doing the show?" I asked eagerly.

"He didn't. I laughed at him when he told me about it. He pleaded with me. He's a huge fan of my dad's, and apparently, I was his first choice when he dreamed up the show. So I told him to call Danny."

"Your cousin?"

"Yeah, he's the son of a rock star, too. And this whole thing is way more his speed. But Danny just opened his own studio, and he didn't have the time to spend eight months gallivanting around the world. So he told Ken he'd talk me into it."

"And he did," I guessed.

"Not without a lot of help. My sister and my Uncle Hank both ganged up on me, too. Then my Aunt Bell, who's a writer herself, thought it was a great way for me to get inspired. And she figured I could write some articles about my travels. Combined with constant calls from Ken, they were wearing me down."

"What did your parents think?" I asked, more than a little curious about the two people who most shaped Henry.

"I don't really know. I mean, they didn't actually tell me. They said I should make my own decision. But I'm pretty sure neither of them thought it was a good idea. In the end, it didn't matter. I needed the money."

"Okay. So I hate to point this out. But you definitely got this job because of your name and your family connections."

"Yeah, I know. But this job isn't even remotely connected to what I actually want to do with my life. And maybe I'm earning the paycheck based on my name, but *I* am still earning it, rather than spending the money my dad earned. So…" He shrugged. "I figured, what the hell. Then I immediately regretted it."

I laughed. "Well, you're stuck now, especially since it appears that we've saved the show."

"I know. Who'd have thought that showing off my nerdiness would help?"

"You, Henry Rushton, are no nerd."

"Oh, yes, I am," he argued.

"I call bullshit. I know what a nerd is. I *am* one. But not you. No way."

"In the morning, the first place I am taking us is to the American Museum of Natural History. And I've been there at least a dozen times before, and most of those times I've been with my *mother*. If that's not nerdy, I don't know what is," he said, leaning toward me, his elbows propped on the table between us.

"Henry," I said, throwing myself into the argument. "A person cannot look like you and be a nerd."

"That is so unfair!" he cried, his eyes sparkling with amusement.

"Look, I admit there are many facets of being a nerd. But one very important one is 'the look,' Henry. A nerd cannot look like"—I waved my hand toward him wildly—"you!"

He pressed his lips together for a moment. "I unequivocally disagree. And that was a two-dollar word, which is worth some major geekdom right there!"

Henry's enthusiasm for our conversation seemed to drain right in front of my eyes as he looked at something across the room. I followed his gaze to see that a news reporter was standing with a photographer in the doorway of the café, scrutinizing us.

"I think you've been made," I told him.

"Damn," he whispered. "We haven't even aired the first episode. See," he said, turning back to me, "this was one of the reasons I didn't want to do this stupid show. It will only get worse. Shit!"

For the first time, I watched Henry unravel in front of me. But before I could dwell on how it made him seem more human, and somehow even more desirable, I jumped into action to help him.

"Let's get out of here," I suggested, scooting out of my side of the booth.

"Good idea." Henry threw a few bills on the table, got up quickly and, to my great surprise, grabbed my hand and pulled me to the door.

We were moving fast as we approached the reporter and photographer. It wasn't until we were squeezing past them in the doorway that the reporter spoke. "Hey, aren't you—"

Henry ignored him and moved his large body so the photographer didn't stand a chance of getting a good shot. Then, still holding onto my hand, he ushered me through the door and out onto the sidewalk. We moved swiftly away from the café, not looking back until we were almost a block away.

"Well done," I said, slowly easing my hand out of Henry's grasp.

Henry held on, giving my fingers a gentle squeeze. "I learned young how to evade the press."

"I bet."

"Where do you want to go?"

I looked at the buildings of Manhattan in the gray hours of early evening. The temperature was starting to drop, but it was still over seventy degrees, and for once, I was quite comfortable in my tank top and light cardigan. I had no qualms about making a long journey. "There," I said, pointing at the Empire State Building.

"All right." Henry's tone was casual. He swung our hands between us as he moved to cross the street.

"It's not too far?"

"Naw. We could always take a cab back."

We were a couple of blocks away from the restaurant, and I was just starting to really obsess over the fact that Henry still held my hand when he started talking. "So, did I prove my point about being a nerd, or do I need to add another piece of evidence?"

"I don't know. I think I'm gonna need to hear about the girlfriends."

"The girlfriends?"

"Yeah. If they're glamorous models or something like that…"

"You think I date models?"

"Quite frankly, Henry. Yes."

"Don't be ridiculous, Chels."

"I'm not," I said defiantly. "I happen to know that your dad dated several models."

"That was all before he met my mom. And I am *not* my dad. I am way nerdier."

"All right, so tell me about your girlfriends."

Henry looked over at me for a moment. Then he smiled. "Fine, nosey. I'll tell you. I started dating in junior high."

"Junior high? Damn."

"Yep. I was young. And I certainly didn't have the self-confidence to ask a girl out. But they were always asking me out. And I simply didn't say no. I had four or five girlfriends at a time. And I got to second base on a regular basis."

"See! Now this is what I expected."

"Wait for the rest of the story, Chels."

"Okay, go on," I said, squeezing his hand.

"By my freshman year in high school, I was turning into a major Casanova. And that's when I got caught. My mom caught me in the bushes behind our house with Tina Grover. She had my dad give me a long lecture. A week later, my Uncle Hank caught me with Heather Green. So *he* gave me a long lecture." He shook his head and let out a low chuckle. "The irony of that…anyway, none of it made a dent. I was fourteen, after all. What *did* make a difference was an incident that took place a few months later. I overheard two of the girls I was seeing talking to each other. I'd caused a lot of trouble between the girls in my class by dating more than one at a time. And I expected them to be fighting over me."

"Good grief," I groaned.

"I know. I know. I was fourteen. Give me a chance to redeem myself here."

"Okay. Go ahead. So they were fighting over you?"

"No. They weren't. That's what was so strange. They knew about each other. And it turned out they had planned together to 'bag me.' I was totally confused. So I asked my cousins Anna and Ella about it. They were the only two girls in my life pretty close to me in age who were not love interests."

"And what did they say?"

"They laughed at me and called me an idiot. They said the reason the girls all wanted to go out with me was because of my famous dad."

"And this hadn't occurred to you before?" I asked, a little flabbergasted.

"I was really stupid back then, okay."

"You were probably just ruled by your hormones," I reasoned.

"Something like that. At any rate, I knew instantly they were right. And I decided to swear off girls. My ego was wrecked. So I took women out of my life altogether. I didn't even have friends who were girls."

"And how long did that last?"

"Until I was a junior in college."

"Wow." I stopped on the sidewalk. "Are you saying you didn't have any girlfriends until your third year of college?"

"Yeah."

"So…you were a virgin until you were, what…twenty-one?"

He bit his lip. "Not exactly."

"But you just said—"

"There were a few women, but they weren't my girlfriends."

"Ah," I said, moving to head back down the sidewalk. "One-night stands."

"Flings, really. I met the first one—you know, the one I lost my virginity to—during a tour with my dad."

"A groupie? You lost your virginity to a groupie! So much for swearing off girls," I teased.

"Well, I was a healthy male going through puberty," he said defensively. Then he stopped and turned to face me, pointing a finger toward me. "When you meet my parents, do not breathe of a word of it. They still don't know."

I laughed, but inside I was thrilled with the idea that Henry had said "*when* you meet my parents." I tugged on his hand so that we started walking again. "Okay, so the first girlfriend. Who was she?"

"Her name was Yasmine. And she hated me at first. She was totally repulsed by me. She thought I was a complete ass."

"Probably because you were."

"Yes. I acted completely standoffish to every woman I wasn't related to. I figured they were all only after me for one reason."

"Super jaded."

"Exactly. So she hated me. And that's what made me want her."

"That makes sense." Sarcasm dripped from my

words.

"It did to me. She was the one woman I knew didn't have ulterior motives to date me. So I set to work to convince her to be with me. It took a while, but eventually it worked. After that, I only dated women who didn't like me."

"Wait, back up," I said. "What happened with Yasmine? How long did it last?"

"Not long. We really didn't have much in common."

"And let me guess. It was the same with the other women."

"Pretty much."

"See, dumbass. That's what you get for dating women who you aren't actually interested in," I said, knocking my elbow against his.

"I know. I'm a complete moron when it comes to dating. I admit it."

"There couldn't have been much passion either with any of these women."

"There wasn't." He shrugged. "I suppose that's why, when I didn't have a girlfriend, I was prone to having the occasional fling."

"You bad boy."

"I suppose you're going to say that takes me out of the running for nerd-dom."

"Nope," I said simply. "Hey, we're closer." I pointed to the Empire State Building with my free hand.

Once again, we came to an abrupt stop on the sidewalk. "No?"

"Not relevant."

"Interesting…So, I am going to assume you are a bit of a bad girl yourself, Chelsea."

"You can assume what you want," I said coyly.

"Oh, come on. I've spilled my guts tonight."

"Okay." I tugged on his hand, and we kept walking. "I've had my fair share of fun. No real boyfriends, though."

"No?"

"Not really. I mean, I guess there were a couple of guys I might have considered boyfriends. But neither of them lasted very long."

"And why's that?"

I shrugged. "I got bored with them easily, I guess."

Henry chuckled. "You and I have a lot in common, Chels. I'm glad I found you."

I swallowed hard. "Yeah?"

"Yeah. I needed a friend." He turned to me. "And I couldn't ask for a better friend on this crazy trip than you."

Chapter 7

Six months and four days ago—New York, New York

"Did you get any last-minute advice from your aunt?" I asked as Tom fitted the microphone on Henry.

"As a matter of fact, I did," Henry told me. "She said to imagine Tyressa is someone else."

"Like Big Bird or something?" Tom asked.

Henry chuckled. "No. Someone who I think is interesting, engaging, and attractive."

"So, who are you going to imagine she is?" I asked.

"Wouldn't you like to know?" Henry wiggled his eyebrows at me and pulled away from Tom to walk over to the table where Tyressa sat, getting a last-minute touch-up on her makeup.

Tom came up behind me and whispered in my ear. "Is it me or was he flirting with you?"

I pushed my glasses up on my nose and focused on the equipment in front of me. "Don't be ridiculous."

Tom snorted but didn't say anything else.

I watched as Henry sat down across from Tyressa and tucked one of her hands in both of his. Just this simple act put me on edge. For the last four days, Henry, Tom, and I had been tromping around the City That Never Sleeps. We went from one site to another, filming, exploring, laughing, and in general enjoying ourselves. And, frequently, as we walked through the city, Henry held my hand. Somehow, watching him hold Tyressa's hand made it all seem cheap.

"Tyressa," Henry cooed. "You look amazing tonight."

I scrambled to move into shooting position and start the camera. I could tell Henry was already in full acting mode.

"Thanks, Henry. You seem to be in a good mood," Tyressa said, smiling brilliantly at him.

"I had a great time exploring New York. How has your week been?"

And just like that, Tyressa and Henry exchanged stories about their New York adventures while I filmed it. And all the while, Henry looked at her like she was interesting, engaging, and attractive.

****

I shut the door behind me and walked straight to the stairwell. It was two floors up to Henry's room, and I bounced up them easily. It was late, around ten or so, and I hadn't seen Henry since after we broke from filming.

I found myself anxious to see him again. My stomach felt tight as I knocked on his door and brooded over the fact I really needed to tamp down my infatuation.

"Chels. What's up?" Henry said, a broad smile on his face as he opened the door.

"Um...hi." It was amazing I was able to get that much out. Henry stood in front of me wearing only a pair of jeans, his bare feet peeking out from beneath the hem. My eyes scanned his tattoos and sculpted pecs, then on down to his washboard abs.

"Come in," he said, moving aside and gesturing to me with his muscular arm.

I ripped my eyes away from his deeply tanned skin and managed to put one foot in front of the other so I could move into the room. I walked over to the loveseat and plopped down roughly on it.

"So, I did it," I announced, looking away from Henry and his tight jeans.

"You did what?" he asked, cocking his head.

I looked him in the eyes. "I met with Snarky Steve just now, and I demanded a raise. And I got it. Now I make *more* money than that little twerp, Jake."

"Chels!" He walked over to the tiny couch and squeezed in beside me. "You did it!" He threw his arms wide and pulled me into a hug.

I soaked it all up, feeling his hard chest against my small breasts, his scratchy cheek against my soft one. I took a deep breath and inhaled his distinct scent.

He pulled me back, his hands still on my shoulders, his back slumped down so he could look me in the eyes. "I am *so* proud of you, Chels!"

I blushed uncontrollably. "Yeah?"

"You didn't even tell me you were going to do it."

I shrugged. "Well, the thing is…I wanted to do it on my own. I wanted to stand up for myself—and my gender—all on my own."

He kissed my cheek. "You are one powerful woman, Chelsea Morrison."

Heat rose from my neck to my hairline, and I was certain my cheeks had turned to beets.

"Let's celebrate." He stood, making me mourn his loss at my side. "This calls for champagne."

My eyes followed Henry as he moved lithely over to the phone and picked up the receiver. "Yeah, champagne sounds good."

****

I rolled over and pulled my hand—which weighed at least thirty pounds—up to my forehead and let out a moan. Too much champagne had me waking up feeling like my head was on fire, my mouth full of cotton, and each one of my limbs tied to a massive boulder.

I managed to drag my eyelids up so I could see my hotel room. Only it wasn't *my* hotel room. My gaze wandered from the painting of a girl with an umbrella on the wall opposite me to the figure lying on the tiny couch beneath it.

Henry was literally twice the size of that couch. Only his upper body was firmly planted on the rough beige upholstery while his long legs were angled between the couch and the thin brown carpeting beside it. Meanwhile, my scrawny-ass self was lying in a massive king-size bed all alone.

I wrenched myself into a sitting position and took a closer look at Henry. His eyes popped open, almost as if he could sense me looking at him. He sat up and ran a hand over his face. He looked sleepy and hungover and absolutely adorable.

"Hi, Wonder Woman," he said, his voice rough. "How are you this morning?"

"I feel like I got run over by a Mack truck. You?"

"Hmm. About the same. Wanna get breakfast?"

"Yeah. I should probably shower first, though," I said, pulling myself off the bed.

I passed Henry on my way to the door. He reached out and took hold of my hand. "Hey, Chels," he said softly, looking up at me.

"Hmm?"

"I might feel like shit right now. But I had a really good time last night. And I am *really, really* proud of you."

I mumbled a thanks and got the hell out of there before I did something really stupid, like propose marriage.

****

Five months ago—Tortola, British Virgin Islands

"You haven't called in two weeks, Chels. We've been worried."

"Says my big brother who disappears for years a time," I groaned.

"God, I will never live that down, will I?" Jack complained.

"Don't let him," I heard Candace say.

"Am I on speakerphone?"

"Yeah, it's Candie's new car. It has the ability to sync you right into the speakers. Isn't that wild?" My brother was clearly floored by this technology.

"Jack, cars have been able to do that for a long time," I told him.

"Not cars I can afford."

Jack had sunk his entire trust fund into his nonprofit and lived hand to mouth. His wife, on the other hand, worked for my dad and made pretty good money. The irony was not lost on any of us.

"Good thing you married rich," I quipped.

"Tell me about it. So, where are you?"

"Hmmm, the Virgin Islands." My voice sounded dreamy, just like it should.

"No kidding?" Candace asked. "How's that?"

"Lovely. The weather is basically everything you ever wished it to be."

"Until a hurricane comes," Jack said.

"Whatever, we'll be gone by then."

"So, are you lying around on the beach and drinking mai tais all day?" Candace asked.

"No. I'm working. But I'm having fun."

"Whoa," Jack said. "You've always liked all the places your job took you to. But I've never heard you say you were *having fun* working."

"Things are different with this gig. Henry, Tom, and I basically have complete creative control over our half of the show. And I barely even see everyone else. It's like the three of us are in our own little bubble."

"So, the hottie turned out to be pretty cool, huh?" As soon as Candace said it I instantly regretted telling her about my crush.

"Hottie?" Jack asked.

"Henry, the rock star's son," Candace told him.

"Last time I tell you a secret, Candace," I griped.

"Sorry, Chelsea." She at least had the grace to sound guilty.

"Are you and this guy…?" Jack stalled out.

"No, Jack. We're just friends. Good friends. Like me and Tom are."

There was a choking sound I was pretty sure came from Candace. "I'm sure it's just like you and Tom," she said sarcastically.

I decided to change the subject as fast as possible. "Whatever. Tell me what's happening at home. How's everyone doing?"

"Jack adopted a dog," Cadence said flatly.

"*We* adopted a dog, and he's adorable," Jack said.

"He's the most pathetic mutt you've ever seen, Chels," Candace told me.

I laughed. I could imagine. Jack was a huge sucker for pathetic. I was about to say exactly that when a knock shook my door. "Hey, guys, I have to go. Someone is here."

"Who?" my big brother asked.

"I don't know. Probably Tom or Steve wanting me to help with some editing."

"Okay, Chelsea. Have fun," Candace said.

"And call again sooner," Jack called.

"Love you," I said just before hanging up.

I walked to the door slowly, sure a long night of looking at film stretched ahead of me. So I was delighted to find Henry on the other side of the door. "Hey, Chelsea," he said as he strode through the door of my hotel room.

I swung the door closed. "What's up?"

"I wanna be outside. It's freaking gorgeous here. And I wanna hang out on the beach, maybe with a bonfire."

"Okay. You looking for company?" I asked, hoping desperately he would tell me that's why he was here, not that he'd come looking for a box of matches or something.

"That's exactly what I'm looking for," he said with a grin.

"Sounds good." I slipped into my sandals. "Who else do you want to invite?"

"No one…I mean, we could ask Tom if you want."

I glanced at the digital clock on the table beside the bed. "It's past his bedtime. At least, for a day he's not cutting film."

"Come on, then," Henry said, holding the door open for me.

Half an hour later, Henry and I sat in lawn chairs on either side of a small gas fire pit, all of which we'd pulled down onto the beach from the hotel's porch.

The sound of waves crashing on the shore complemented the creaking of chairs as we shifted and the strange soft sound of the fake fire. There was no wind, and the still, warm air felt like a hug as it surrounded me. I looked at Henry, sitting just a few feet away, and in that moment, I was utterly content.

"Well, it isn't exactly like the bonfires I remember growing up. But it'll do," he said, giving a sour look to the little metal dish burning orange flames in front of us.

"Hmmm. You'll have to regale me so I can live vicariously. Not a lot of sitting out on the beach in San Francisco."

"Too damn cold," he said, stretching his long legs out in front of me.

"And windy."

"Hmmm."

"So, come on. Tell me what it was like growing up in a mansion in Malibu," I urged.

"First of all, it isn't a mansion. It's just a house. I've seen the place you grew up in on freaking magazine covers, Chels. *That* is a mansion."

"One magazine cover, once. And why on earth were you looking at that magazine?"

"My mom had it. And the point is, my parents' house is practically a hovel compared to that thing."

"Okay, but their 'hovel' is in Malibu," I pointed out.

"True."

"I'm waiting."

Henry gazed into the fire and began his description. "We have a pretty substantial backyard with a pool. A path winds through some trees and bushes out to the beach. Sometimes we set up in the backyard, other times on the beach. It just depends on the privacy factor. At any rate, we'd set up a big bonfire. A real one with actual wood," he said, gesturing dismissively to the flames in front of us. "And we have a bunch of chairs, lawn chairs, camp chairs, all different. But"—he held his finger up—"at least half the chairs are those 'big man' chairs."

"Yeah, that's right. Because you come from a family of giants."

"Only on one side. But, yes," he agreed.

"So you all sit around a fire. And you do what? The adults talk, the kids make s'mores?" I asked, picturing it perfectly in my head.

"Yes, and usually at the end of the night, it breaks out into a jam session."

"Jam session?"

"Yeah, guitars come out, and my dad and Hank sing." He chuckled and got a faraway look in his eye. "When we were kids, my sister would fall asleep in my mom's lap and I would fight to stay awake." He leaned back in his chair and looked up at the sky. "I love that backyard."

I sat up straighter in my chair. "So, you have to tell me, Henry. Do you play guitar?"

It was a closely guarded secret. I must have overheard other people on the show ask Henry this question a million times in the past three months. But he never answered it. He was a master of evasion. I wondered if he would answer me now.

"Can you keep a secret?" he asked.

"Of course I can."

"I can play. I learned to play on a ukulele before I could spell my own name."

"Then why the hell is it such a big secret?" I asked, sitting forward in my chair to stare at him across the fire pit.

Henry was still leaned back, his gaze fixed on the stars above. "Well, it's like this, Chels. I play for fun. I'm not particularly good. At least not good enough to make a living at it. And I wouldn't want to even if I was. I like to play with my dad and my uncles around a fire in the backyard or in the living room, but that's it. When people find out I can play, they all want me to do it for them. But it's something I do only when surrounded by my family. It's personal. You know?"

"I think I get that. It's too bad I won't get to hear you play, though."

"I'll play for you some day, Chels," he said casually.

"You will?" I asked, surprised.

"Sure. You're practically family."

I went completely still as I digested this. Henry gazed up at the stars as if he hadn't said anything extraordinary. Our close friendship shouldn't be in any way surprising. After all, Henry and I had spent sixteen to eighteen hours a day together for the last three months. We were the same age. We had the same dry sense of humor and tendency to overuse sarcasm. And we shared an understanding of the first world problems of growing up a rich kid.

I felt the same as Henry, ninety percent of the way at least. Except while I was comfortable in his presence, enjoyed his company, and valued his friendship, I also deeply desired his body. In fact, if I could stop dreaming and fantasizing about him and me naked in bed, in the back seat of a car, or in a stairwell, we'd be in good shape.

"What are you thinking about over there?" Henry asked me.

Unable to tell him the truth, I made something up quickly. "Um…that hot island waiter from dinner."

"Huh. You little vixen. Did you get his number?"

"No. I don't think a guy like that has a geek fetish."

He rolled his head on the back of the chair, shifting his focus from the sky to me. "Oh, please, Chels. You're hot, and you know it. And that dude was definitely looking."

I had no idea where to take this conversation. I pushed up my glasses while I contemplated that. Finally, I said, "Well, maybe I'm not so good at figuring out who's interested." My chest constricted as I said it. This ridiculous, secret hope crept up in me that Henry would say, "I'm interested, Chels." Then I would leap out of my chair and into his arms.

I shook my head to clear it of the fantasy and paid attention to what Henry was saying to me.

"Don't worry. I got your back."

"Yeah?" I managed to respond as my dream died a terrible death.

"Yeah, I'll be your spotter. I'll tell you when a guy's interested."

This wouldn't be weird if he were any other friend of mine. It wouldn't be weird if it were Tom, Candace, or even my college buddy, Greg. So, why was it weird now? "You'd do that for me?" I asked.

"What are friends for?"

Chapter 8

Four months ago—Rio de Janeiro, Brazil

"Come here, gorgeous!" Meno cried as he scooped me up into a massive bear hug.

After a couple more stops in the Caribbean and a few more in South America, we were closing the Western Hemisphere in Rio de Janeiro, the town where my big brother had once hidden for five years. His best friend, Meno, still lived here. And while I'd only seen Meno in person twice, he'd promised Jack he'd take care of me while I was in Brazil. Not one to shirk his responsibilities, Meno met us at the airport when we landed.

"Hey," I said, accepting his embrace easily. "Good to see you again."

Meno pulled back and looked at me. He was truly one of the kindest, most sincere people I'd ever met, but he was a serious flirt. "My God, Chelsea, if you weren't my best friend's sister. Mmmmm."

"Stop it, Meno," I said, slapping his shoulder.

"Welcome to winter!" he said, laughing. "Must be strange to go from summer in the states to winter down here."

I was only half paying attention to Meno because I was looking around at the rest of the cast and crew. I'd come off the plane last, and they were all either dealing with our gear or looking at maps. In Tyressa's case, she was on the phone. In Henry's case, he was talking to two people I'd never seen before. The three of them stood in a corner of the room. I squinted my eyes to get a better look.

Meno was saying something about how it was still pretty warm here, and I wouldn't need a coat or anything. Finally, he reclaimed my attention. "Chelsea."

I turned back to him. "Sorry, Meno." I smiled. "I was just thinking about where we are headed next."

"What are your plans?"

I shrugged. "We have tomorrow off. Tomorrow night is the airing of the first episode of the show. And then we get to work the next morning. So I'm free until then."

"Good." Meno rubbed his hands together. "Because I have plans for us."

"Chels!" I turned to see Henry gesturing to me from across the room. "Come here for a sec, will you."

I grabbed Meno's hand and dragged him with me as I approached Henry. I assumed the man beside him was his cousin Danny. I knew Danny planned to meet up with us in Rio. The man stood tall, like Henry, but aside from that, they shared absolutely no similarities in their appearance. Not that they should. Danny was the son of Hank Tolk, Henry's dad's best friend. They weren't actually related. So it wasn't strange that the fairer, thinner, lighter-haired man didn't look like his cousin.

I had no idea, however, who the woman was beside Danny. As I neared the trio, I could see she was one of those impossibly beautiful women. She stood quite a bit shorter than me, maybe five foot three inches, and I knew from experience a lot of men found that cute, unlike my above-average height of five foot ten inches. She had curves in all the right places, unlike me, who had no curves at all. And she had long, beautiful, flowing, straight-as-an-arrow blonde hair.

Worst of all, I knew she couldn't be Danny's girlfriend because Henry had already told me Danny was gay. Actually, his exact words had been, "He bats for the same team as Tom." At the time his statement had led to a sentimental conversation about the LGBTQ people in our lives and what they meant to us. Now it was hitting me in the face because I knew this girl was not necessarily taken.

"Hey, Chels. This is Danny," Henry said excitedly.

"Hi, Danny," I said, shaking his hand.

"And this is Danny's BFF, Erika," he said, gesturing to gorgeous.

I shook her hand, too, while Danny said, "Chelsea Morrison. I've heard a lot about you."

"Oh yeah?" I wanted to explore that statement further, but I felt Meno's elbow dig into my ribs. I quickly recovered. "Um, Henry, Danny, Erika, this is Meno." I wasn't entirely sure how to introduce Meno, and I hadn't mentioned him to Henry at all. So I went with vague. Meno shook hands with each of them and gave them his ever-charming smile.

"You're American," Henry noted.

"Yep. Chelsea's big brother, Jack, and I were college roommates. I moved down here a few years back."

"And now he owns his own restaurant," I told them, pushing my glasses up on my nose.

"I was about to take Chelsea to my place for dinner. You all interested in joining us?" Meno added with a smile.

****

All through dinner, I'd watched with rapt attention at the activity taking place across the table from me. Erika was not only gorgeous, she was also charming, sophisticated, and flirty as hell. And the primary focus of her affectionate attention was Henry.

I'd managed to make it through the meal by keeping a near constant flow of wine down my throat. So, when Henry, Danny, and Erika finally said goodnight and headed off into the Rio night, Meno cut me off.

"I've never seen you drunk before, Chelsea," he said, pulling the wine bottle straight out of my hands. "Since your brother makes you sound like a saint, I kinda wondered if you even did drink."

"My brother is delusional," I told him, looking around the restaurant for the first time in hours. "Hey, where is everybody?"

"The place is closed. That's why my staff cleaned up everything but this table." Meno gestured to the table in front of us, littered with the remains of our feast.

I swung my head around and took in the spotless tables all around me, covered in clean linens and awaiting tomorrow's customers. "Wow. I suppose it's late."

Meno chuckled. "What's up with you?"

I refocused on him. "What do you mean?"

Meno leaned forward on his elbows, his bushy, dark brown eyebrows raised. "I mean, something is up with you."

I avoided his gaze and waved a hand dismissively at him.

"Okay," he said, leaning back in his chair and placing his hands behind his head. "I'll just ask Jack why you're acting so strange.

My gaze instantly snapped up. I watched the smirk play on Meno's face. He knew he'd just won.

"I've got a thing for Henry, all right?" I said defensively.

"Hmmm. And?"

"And what?"

"You're jealous of that Erika chick?"

"Duh."

"That makes no sense."

Now I was frustrated, which along with the wine and my already irritated state, made me sound pretty pissy. "How *exactly* does that *not* make sense?"

"If you've got a thing for the guy, why are you pining over him and watching him flirt with other chicks? Why aren't you taking action?"

I pouted at him, unsure of how truthful I wanted to be. "He's my friend. I don't want to ruin—"

"Bullshit," Meno interrupted.

My mouth flew open, and I stared at him.

"That's bullshit," he repeated. "What's the real reason?"

"Uh, uh" I stuttered.

"Okay, let me guess. You think he's out of your league." My mouth managed to drop even farther, and Meno winked. "Knew it. That's total crap, Chelsea. You're a beautiful, intelligent, desirable woman."

"Thanks. I appreciate that. But if he's already with

someone else…"

"You think he's already with this chick and she's here on long-distance booty call and he never once mentioned it to you?"

The tone of Meno's voice made it clear he thought it sounded ridiculous when repeated back. But I wasn't so sure. There was something in Erika's behavior that spoke to familiarity. And there was definitely something in the way she looked at me that said "competition."

"Why don't you just ask him?" Meno suggested.

"Ask him if he's hooking up with Erika?"

"Sure, and if he is, ask him what she means to him."

I wished I could be that straightforward. Maybe it said something about my friendship with Henry that I couldn't. Hell, I could be completely blunt with my brother's best friend. Why couldn't I be the same with my own?

****

Two months and two weeks ago—Paris, France

By the time we were tromping through Europe, the events in Rio left far behind us, Henry and I were back to being whatever it was we were. In fact, during our time in Europe, we'd grown even closer. We'd started to have long talks every evening as we wound down from our busy days. We'd walked through the streets of European towns side by side and often hand in hand. Our physical closeness had prompted Tom to ask me, pointedly, if Henry and I were sleeping together. When I'd explained we were just good friends, he'd clucked his tongue and shook his head at me.

Through all of this, I'd basically been playing mind

games with myself. I'd tried to convince myself our friendship was just a special one and there weren't any rules to it. I'd also told myself I wasn't sexually attracted to Henry anymore. I'd tried to convince myself if confronted with a situation like the one with Erika again, I wouldn't be jealous. I also found new excuses to not bring Erika up as I'd told Meno I would.

The events in Paris forced me to confront how deeply I'd lied to myself.

On our second night there, I arranged to meet up with my friend, Charles. It wasn't a big deal, but for some reason, I didn't want to discuss who Charles was or what he meant to me with Henry. So I'd planned to go without mentioning it to him.

After we'd finished shooting for the day, we went straight to the hotel. It was a hot day, and we all wanted a shower. As I got dressed, I ignored the text message Henry sent me asking about dinner plans. I felt a little guilty as I put my phone on vibrate and shoved it in my pocket before leaving my room and heading to the hotel lobby. I was halfway to the front door when I spotted Henry sitting on a couch in the center of the spacious room, looking right at me.

He stood as I approached. "There you are." Henry smiled at me and ran a hand through his damp hair. He looked hotter than hell and smelled like an ad for some fancy, manly soap.

"Hi."

"Did you want to get dinner?"

"Actually, I'm meeting up with a friend, who lives here in Paris, for dinner…You could join us, you know, if you want to."

"I didn't know you had a friend in Paris," he said,

cocking his head to one side.

I shrugged. "I guess I didn't mention him...um, he was a contractor we hired for a show we did last year."

"And?" Henry raised one eyebrow.

I blushed and looked down at the floor. This should not be so hard. It should not be difficult to tell this to my best friend. But, for some reason, I really struggled. "We had a fling. But you know. We're just friends now."

"Well, in that case, you'd better go alone," Henry said, grinning.

My head snapped up, and I looked at him. "Oh no," I protested quickly. "It's not like that."

Henry rolled his eyes. "Please, Chels. Go get laid. You don't need me hanging around."

I felt like a balloon that had just been pricked with a needle. I didn't know why, but I hated the idea Henry was so damned happy about me having sex with someone else. I walked away feeling more hurt than I could ever have anticipated.

Chapter 9

Present day—Los Angeles, California
Henry

I look over at my father. He is sitting across from me. His arms are folded over his chest, and there is a deep crease in his brow.

"Well?" I ask him. I'm halfway through my story, and he hasn't said a word, not that this surprises me. But now I want some feedback.

"Well what?" he asks me.

I roll my eyes. "At this point, Chelsea and I were just friends. We were close. I'd never had a friend like her in my life. I was comfortable with her and happy around her. Our relationship was freaking perfect. I couldn't see any of this shit coming, Dad."

My dad is well aware of the fact something terrible has gone wrong between Chelsea and me. He knew it the moment he saw me tonight. But I haven't yet explained to him exactly what went wrong. Instead, he'd asked me to start the story at the beginning, when I'd first met Chelsea. And for the last twenty minutes, I'd been doing just that. Now I am at a turning point in my tale, and I want to know what he's thinking so far.

"Hmmm," he mumbles.

"Do you think I should have?" I ask.

"Seen it coming?"

"Yes!" My frustration is definitely showing.

But my dad, a consummate Zen master, is perfectly calm. "Not necessarily. I mean, you *didn't* see it coming, Buddy. It is what it is."

I pull out the leather tie, and my hair flops down around my shoulders. I run my hands through it absentmindedly. "I just feel like, if I could have seen what was about to happen…"

"What would you have done differently?"

That is a good question. I stroke my three-day-old stubble and contemplate it. What *would* I have done differently? "I guess I should have asked her how she felt about our friendship," I suggest.

My dad waves his hand at me dismissively. "No way. That is completely unlikely. No one would have a conversation that weird for no reason."

"Right. See? There isn't anything. Damn it!"

My dad unfolds his arms and leans forward. His massive tattooed forearms rest on his knees. His hair, which is almost identical to mine save for a handful of thin streaks of gray, slides around his shoulders. "It's what happened later that *I'm* interested in."

"I'm not even sure how to tell that part of the story."

"Why don't you start with the first time *you* knew things were changing between you?" he suggests.

I let out a heavy sigh. "I guess it was in France."

My dad leans back in his chair, settling in for the rest of my story. "Hmmm. What happened in France?"

****

Two months and two weeks ago—Paris, France

Chelsea walked away from me. My eyes followed her. She wore her favorite pair of jeans. They were worn in several places and fit her so perfectly my gaze was naturally drawn to her curves. She wasn't wearing a T-shirt with Woodsy the Owl or Princess Leia on it, as she usually did. That night she had on a tight-fitting, blue cotton top that showed off the creamy skin between the bottom of her neck and the subtle V just above the lace of her bra, which peeked out the tiniest bit above the thin material of the light-colored blouse.

She looked freaking amazing, and I'd just sent her off to get laid. The thought made my chest tight.

Our conversation had taken place in the lobby of the hotel. I'd been about to ask her to go have dinner with me when she'd told me about her date with Charles. I sat down on a couch behind me, dropping my body roughly to a sitting position while at the same time watching Chelsea disappear through the front door.

Something was going on with me. I was uncomfortable, unhappy, and super tense. I realized I had two options. I could figure out why I felt this way, or I could completely ignore it and go about my business. I sat there in limbo for several minutes, not wanting to make a choice. Then Tom walked out of the elevator and approached me. He provided exactly the distraction I needed.

I stood. "Hey, Tom."

"What's up, Henry? Where's Chelsea?" he asked.

"She went out. Wanna grab dinner with me?"

"Sure." Tom held out his arm and indicated for me to lead the way.

We stepped out onto the sidewalk in front of the hotel. I looked around for Chelsea instinctively as we made our way out into the open. I spotted her at the curb, just ducking into a cab. She looked up at me, pausing for a moment. Her body was in mid-motion, her knees bent, her torso angled toward the cab. Her head stuck up over the top of the car door, and she caught my eyes. Her brow creased, her lips pulled tight. Then, without any further acknowledgement of me, she disappeared into the car. The cab left the curb and merged into traffic, blending into the fabric of vehicles on the road.

Tom did not, apparently, see any of this. He pulled on my arm and pointed toward a sign at the end of the block. "Let's go to that place. The front desk clerk told me it was good."

I nodded and followed him.

I waited until Tom and I were done with our meal and waiting on dessert to be brought before bringing up Chelsea. "Can I ask you something?" I leaned toward him, my elbows on the table.

"I was wondering when you'd get around to it," he said, grinning.

"What do you mean?" I asked, my brow scrunching up in confusion.

"You have clearly been chewing something over through this entire meal. I've been dying to ask you about it, but I figured it was only a matter of time before you came out with it. It looks like my patience paid off."

"Huh," I said, suddenly even more hesitant to reveal what was on my mind.

"Henry. Where's Chelsea?" he asked, looking at me pointedly.

"She went out on a date," I said, sounding very much like a pouty child.

"A date?"

"Yeah, with some guy named Charles."

"Oh." He leaned back in his seat. "Charles."

"You know this guy?" I asked, unable to contain my interest.

"Yeah, they had a whirlwind fling last year. You know, one of those fun, romantic European hook-ups." He was talking slowly, examining my expression with each and every word.

I took a sip of my beer, feeling a little like I was in a weird dream, and sat back myself, trying to imitate his casual demeanor. "Sure. I'm familiar with the concept." I gave him a playboy grin, the kind my cousin Danny was a master of.

Tom scrutinized me, clearly unconvinced by my body language. "So, uh, no worries, huh?"

"Worries? About what?"

"Chelsea, off with some dude…"

"She's a big girl." I looked away from him as I said it, scanning the room. I spotted a woman a few tables away from us. She stared at me hard. When our eyes met, she smiled. I held her gaze and nodded my head. "Maybe I'll take her example myself," I told Tom, trying to channel Danny again.

Out of the corner of my eye, I saw Tom swivel his head to follow my gaze. "Is that right?" Skepticism dripped from his voice.

"Yeah."

"You never did ask me whatever it was you were going to ask me," he pointed out.

I kept my gaze on the woman nearby. "It was nothing." In truth, he'd already answered my question. I wanted to know about Chelsea and Charles. And now that he'd confirmed my fears, I just felt sick. I wanted to get away from this conversation, this situation, all of it. I wanted to get rid of this feeling in my gut. So I stood. "I don't mean to be rude, but I think I'm gonna excuse myself."

"Sure. Go," he said, waving his hand at me. "I got the company credit card. I'll take care of the bill."

I walked slowly over to the woman. She sat at a small square table with two girlfriends. All three went quiet as I approached.

I was absolutely no good at this. But somehow, I managed to keep up the Danny act long enough to get invited to sit with them. The woman who'd smiled at me was beautiful in a classical sense. She had a thick, rich accent to her English. Her name was Yvonne, and she looked like she belonged on a runway somewhere.

Yvonne laughed at everything I said, tossing back her shiny, smooth black hair and exposing the spotless, perfectly tanned skin of her long neck. She pivoted in her chair just so, allowing me to see her long, perfectly sculpted legs from the tops of her feet, which were tucked into four-inch heels, to the bottom of the short, well-fitting dress that hugged all her curves.

But I wasn't interested, not in the least. That problem I had no answer for, just as I had no answer for my feelings about Chelsea and her date. So I waited until Tom had left the restaurant, with one last wave toward me, before making some lame excuse and getting the hell out of there myself.

As I took the stairs back up to my hotel room, I decided I would have to face my issues sooner or later. In no hurry to do so, I went back to my room and threw myself into writing an article about our travels through

Europe.

The writing was a great way to occupy my mind. However, I found that as I wrote, I described Chelsea and all my adventures with her in great detail. After hours of typing frantically, I reread what I'd written. It was chock full of descriptions of Chelsea's beautiful blue eyes, her soft, smooth skin, and the adorable way she pushed her glasses up on her nose, even when they weren't falling down.

I closed my laptop in frustration and went to bed.

Chapter 10

Two months, five days ago—Dublin, Ireland

It had been nine days since Chelsea's date in Paris. I hadn't brought it up, and neither had she. But I still thought about it all the time.

"I can't believe it," Chelsea said, pushing her glasses up on her nose. "I mean this building is over *eight hundred years old*. Our whole freaking country is…less than a third that old."

I wasn't looking at St. Patrick's Cathedral in front of me. I watched Chelsea. She was so stinking cute when she geeked out. "Not really," I said, trying to get a rise out of her. "People have been living on the North American continent for thousands—"

"All right, jackass. You knew what I meant," she said, hitting me playfully on the arm while keeping her gaze on the building in front of us.

"You wanna go in? Or are we just going to stare at it from out here?" I asked.

"Shut up."

We'd already shot all of our Dublin footage. It focused on two separate pub crawls, one on the literary greats of Ireland and one on the musical geniuses of the small island country. This trip to the cathedral was just for our own amusement.

I grabbed Chelsea's hand and led her toward the

massive double wooden doors that stood like ancient guardians to the historic stone structure. "Come on, history geek. Let's check this out."

Chelsea never objected when I took her hand. In fact, she seemed to expect it these days. And she should, because I was always doing it. I couldn't seem to help myself. I always wanted to be close to Chelsea.

When we sat in my hotel room in the evenings and watched TV, I usually had an arm around her shoulder, and I frequently found myself gently rubbing circles on her upper arm with my fingers.

"All right," she said, tugging on my hand. She pulled me out of my thoughts and through the impressive arch.

Chelsea dragged me through the building, showing me the elaborate sculptures, stained glass windows and tombs. I looked at the sights and took a few pictures with my phone. History interested to me. But, for the first time, I was *more* interested in watching how my companion reacted to everything *she* saw.

It had been nine days since Chelsea's date with Charles, and eight days since I'd admitted to myself I was jealous about it. I still didn't know what the hell was happening to me.

****

Two months ago—London, England

"What do you want to do for our last night in Europe?" I asked Chelsea.

"I want to drink too much hard cider."

I smirked at her. "So, Chelsea wants to let her hair down."

"Yep." She nodded her head vigorously. "I've been working hard, and I'll be busting my ass again once we get to the other side of the pond, too. Tonight, it's all about me and getting a good buzz on."

"You wanna head to a pub?"

"Nope. I don't want to have to deal with that. Besides this country is stupid cold, even in August." Poor Chelsea was always chilly. English weather was not at the top of her list. "I want to get a bunch of cider and get blasted right here in my very nice, very warm hotel room. That way I can just crash out at the end of the night, no cab ride needed."

I laughed. "I'm in. I'll order the cider." I picked up the phone that sat on the bedside table.

"Order?" she asked from her spot on the king-size bed a few feet away from me.

"Sure. They have room service."

"From the bar?"

I narrowed my eyes. "I thought you grew up rich? You should know you can get anything delivered to your room...for a price," I teased.

She shrugged. "I guess. But you and me, we aren't rich anymore, at least as long we refuse to touch those trust funds."

"True. But the show is covering all our expenses now."

She grinned. "I like the way you think, Henry."

After the booze was delivered, we watched three episodes of the British *The Office* and had a hard cider per episode. Then, the conversation we'd been having comparing the original to the American version of the show took an unexpected turn.

It all started with a cryptic comment from Chelsea. "See now, on the American version, Pam always gave me hope."

"Hope?" I asked.

We were both sitting on her bed, our backs propped against the headrest and our legs out in front of us. She stared at our bare feet, peeking up beside each other at the end of the bed, as she explained. "She's a regular girl. I mean, she's pretty and all. But she's a regular girl, and she finds Jim and her happily-ever-after. And it's like, everyone can do that, no matter who they are. You don't have to look like Julia Roberts."

"You worried you won't find your happily-ever-after, Chels?" I teased.

"Sure. Isn't everyone?"

The seriousness in her voice surprised me. "You're young, kid. You've got time."

"Hey," she said, looking up at me. "You are exactly the same age as me."

"Not true. I'm three and half months older," I pointed out.

"Whatever." She turned to face the television again and took a drink of cider number four. I was pretty sure she was quite buzzed at this point, and I hoped that would bring out the honesty. It always seemed to work that way for me. "Not the point," she said. "And you wouldn't understand, anyway. You're not a regular person."

"What?" I asked, incredulous. I muted the television, then turned my body so I fully faced her. "I thought we established—"

"We established that you are a nerd. But you are still a very *hot* nerd," she interrupted. "I think Erika proved that."

"Erika?" I asked, confused.

"That girl is gorgeous, and she is way out of the

league of the average nerd."

What the hell? "You think I hooked up with Erika?"

She turned to face me then. "Didn't you?"

I couldn't help but smile. Maybe she was jealous, and for some reason, the thought tickled me silly. "I don't want to kiss and tell."

She punched me lightly on the arm. "You can tell me."

"I suppose it doesn't count when you tell your best friend."

"No, it doesn't," she agreed.

"We didn't hook up," I admitted.

"No? Why not?"

I shrugged and took a long swig from my bottle of cider. In truth, I was feeling a little buzzed at the moment, as well, and I risked too much honesty.

"Seriously, Henry. Why not?" she pressed.

"She's not really my speed."

"Your speed? What on earth does that mean?"

I shrugged again. "I don't really know. But she just wasn't for me. And she was too eager."

Her mouth dropped open. "What the hell does that mean? You only want a girl who plays hard to get? That's kinda fucked up, you know."

"No." I elbowed her lightly in the ribs. "That's not it, and you know it. I'm just always questioning girls' motives. And as a result, when a girl crawls all over me on sight I have to be suspicious."

"I thought she was your cousin's best friend. So, one, haven't you known her for a while? And two, doesn't that kinda change her motives?"

"She and Danny are *fast* friends, like me and you.

They just met last year. Rio was only the second time I'd ever hung out with her. And I definitely question her motives, especially when it comes to me. There's something…"

"You're jaded," she teased.

"Maybe. Maybe I'm just careful."

"Yeah, well, it's preventing you from getting laid."

I chuckled. She was right about me not getting laid. She was wrong about the reason. "Teach me, oh wise one. You know how to keep your bed warm. How do you do it?"

As soon it popped out of my mouth, my heart started to race. Yes, I wanted to know what had happened between her and Charles, and going back further, her and Meno. But I wasn't entirely sure I could handle it, especially in this state of lowered inhibitions.

"What?" she shouted, shoving herself up on her knees and placing her bottle of cider on the table beside the bed. She appeared to be ready for a fight. "What the hell does that mean?"

"Hey, don't get mad. I only speak the truth." I threw my arms up in surrender.

"Again, what?"

"Chels, you've had two different dudes in the last few months," I pointed out. "I'm not judging. I stand in admiration."

"I have not!"

"Meno and that dude in France," I said, a touch of *gotcha* in my tone.

She dropped down onto her butt so we were facing each other. "Oh. You think me and Meno had a thing?"

"That's what it looked like to me," I admitted.

"Well, we didn't."

"No?" I asked, surprised and definitely pleased.

"No. He's my big brother's best friend. I would think it was too weird, and he'd be scared of Jack, with reason, I might add."

"Well, you two seemed quite cozy."

"He was just..." She paused, biting her lip and shifting her gaze away from me.

I looked at her expectantly. "Yeah?"

"I don't know. Meno's just a flirt."

"What about Charles?" I probed.

Her eyes snapped back to mine, and she grinned. "I admit I had a fling with Charles last year when I was in town on a shoot. But not this time. We just went out and had a drink. He has a girlfriend now. Besides, I wasn't as interested this time."

I suddenly felt like a huge weight had been lifted off my shoulders. Chelsea hadn't actually been with anyone this entire time. "Hmmm," I mumbled, relaxing myself further. "Why not?"

"I don't know."

"What changed from last year that made you no longer interested?"

"Why the third degree about this?" She leaned toward me, and I leaned toward her. We sat on her bed, half-drunk, our faces maybe four or five inches from each other. I could *feel* how close she was to me.

"I'm curious," I said softly, my gaze dancing between her eyes and her plump lips.

"He doesn't do it for me anymore," she said, her voice sounding low and hoarse.

"No?" I reached up and pulled the glasses off her face. I folded the arms in and set them beside me on the table without ever taking my eyes off her.

"No." She was practically whispering now. "My tastes have changed."

"Yeah? What do you like now?" I asked, placing one hand on her waist.

"Dark brown eyes," she said, staring into my mine.

"Hmmm. What else?" My other hand moved to the back of her neck.

"Long black hair," she said. She reached up, her left hand drifting into my hair.

"Hmmm," I mumbled, just before pulling her head gently with my hand until my lips were pressed to hers.

She sighed, and her mouth fell open. I opened my own mouth and deepened our kiss. She angled her head. I pulled her waist toward me while the hand on her neck moved into her hair. As I pulled her silky locks through my fingers, she reached out to me with her tongue. This move increased my enthusiasm. I reared up on my knees, then pushed her gently onto her back, following her down until I hovered over her.

She slid her hands down my back and sides, which I absolutely loved. Then she tugged on the waist of my jeans. It took me by surprise, and my muscles gave way, pulling me down on top of her. I managed to readjust my weight to keep it off her, all the while still kissing her like crazy.

I groaned and pulled my mouth back just enough to speak. "Chels, you are…" Unable to find the word I was looking for, I plunged my mouth back into hers.

My hands roamed, and so did Chelsea's. But our mouths stayed locked together. I wasn't willing to stop tasting her, and she must have felt exactly the same way because she didn't pull away, not for a second.

I had no idea how long we stayed like that, making

out like a pair of horny teenagers. Eventually, my roaming fingers made their way into her jeans and under her panties, exactly where I wanted to be.

I was completely attuned to Chelsea as I stroked her, kissed her, and inhaled her scent. I knew she was getting closer and closer to climax. Then she ripped her mouth away from mine. I turned my lips and tongue to her neck while she gasped and moaned and yelled, "Jesus, Henry!"

My stomach rippled as she cried out my name. I reluctantly pulled my hand back and smiled down at her.

"You look pretty proud of yourself," she said, stretching languidly.

"Oh, I am," I told her, propping my head up above her with my hand, my elbow on the bed beside her cheek.

"What now? We just went at each other like rabbits."

"We'll talk about it in the morning."

"Really? That's your solution?" she asked, a touch of incredulity in her tone.

"Yeah. We're too drunk to have a rational conversation now. But"—I pulled myself off her—"not so drunk we'll really fuck up."

I knew better than to go any farther. And I knew Chelsea did, too. So I wasn't surprised when she agreed. "Okay. So we'll talk about it tomorrow. But you have to promise it won't be weird."

I stood up beside the bed, desperate to get out of there. The longer I stayed, the more I would want.

"I promise." I leaned down and gave her a quick kiss on the lips.

I knew we'd have to talk about all of this sooner or later. But I wasn't in any hurry to do it. And I had more pressing needs. I stood and her eyes went to the bulge in my jeans, which was now directly in front of her.

"In the meantime, I need a cold shower," I told her.

The truth was, I needed to be alone so I could fantasize about what I really wanted to do with Chelsea and take care of this bulge without the guilt of having done it with my half-drunk best friend.

I leaned down once more to kiss her forehead. "Night, Chels."

Chapter 11

Present day—San Francisco, California
Chelsea

I bite my lip and look up at Jack. As I expected, he's making a face. I roll my eyes and turn to Candace. She waves a hand dismissively at him. "Ignore him. This is an important part of the story."

"Ugh," Jack finally says.

"Whatever, Jack. It's not like you were a virgin when I found you," Candace says.

I laugh.

"Not the same," he protests.

I roll my eyes again.

"Okay, so," Candace says, adjusting herself in her seat. "You were 'intimate' in London." She makes air quotes with her fingers. "But you were both a little tipsy."

"Yeah, but I think it had been building for a while, at least for me."

"I'm sure that road went both ways," Candace says.

"I hate to even talk about this, but I agree," Jack says.

"Yeah?" I question.

"Did you honestly think you were the only one feeling the attraction?" Candace asks me.

"Well, yes. I did. At least at that point."

Jack is staring at me like I've just spoken in ancient Greek.

"You wouldn't understand a dorky girl's basic sense of low self-esteem when confronted with a beautiful and perfect specimen of a man," I tell him.

"No, he wouldn't," Candace says. "But *I* do."

I rolled my eyes because Candace is basically a cover model for Vanity Fair as far as I am concerned. Of course, she doesn't see it that way. I complain about being boney. She complains about having too much excess around the middle. We both know we should love our bodies for what they are. And we both know what a great idea that is in theory, but not so practical all the time in reality.

Candace ignores the face I'm making because she's completely used to it and says, "So. You two got frisky at the hotel in London. What happened next?"

****

One month, three weeks, six days ago—Boston, Massachusetts

We'd taken a commercial flight back to the US on a great big jet. Henry and I had managed to sit in the same row, but we had Tom beside us and Gerry in the row in front of us. It hadn't exactly been conducive to having a conversation about our accidental drunken make-out session.

The time together, but not alone, had been therapeutic, at least for me. From the moment Henry had left my room the night before, I'd been stressed out over what we'd done. I valued my friendship with Henry in a way I'd never treasured any other friendship in my life. I didn't want to risk harming it in any way.

So I'd stayed up most of the night worrying about the consequences of our actions.

On the plane, however, we'd easily fallen back into our previous arrangement. We'd been just Henry and Chelsea again. We'd laughed, we'd teased, we'd caused everyone around us to groan and roll their eyes at our antics. And I'd completely relaxed again, my stress nearly forgotten.

But the conversation Henry and I desperately needed to have had not left my mind. So once we were settled in our hotel in Boston that night, I went to Henry's room. It was late, and everyone was jetlagged. So, knowing the rest of the crew would be in their rooms, I asked Henry to go with me to the hotel bar so we could talk.

He looked at me strangely when I asked, and I knew why. We usually preferred to stay in one of our rooms alone, talking into the night. But I didn't want to be alone with Henry again just yet. So we sat on either side of a small table in the thickening quiet of the bar, having a drink and trying to complete our awkward conversation before last call.

"I just think we need to talk about it," I said quietly, leaning toward Henry as if we were discussing a bank robbery.

"If you say so, Chels. I've never really had a close friend before who was a girl, let alone…this. So, you tell me. What's the sitch?"

"I've had two friends with benefits, Henry. I'm no stranger to the concept."

He leaned forward, propping his forearms on the table before us. "Okay, and how did that go?"

"One went well, and one not so well."

"Tell me about them."

"My friend Gary and I had a thing. We were friends, and we slept together occasionally." I stopped for a moment, swallowing hard. Henry and I had not slept together, and the idea hadn't even been broached until now. But I continued on. "And then Gary got a girlfriend. We stopped sleeping together, and we just went back to being friends. He told his girlfriend about us, and she was cool with it. In fact, she and I became good friends."

"And the other one?" he asked.

I let out a heavy sigh. "His name was Roger. And he and I were friends with bennies for about six months. But he wanted to date, and I didn't. So I insisted we end it. And he didn't take it well. We haven't spoken since."

"Okay, but were either of them like us?" he asked, taking my hand in his across the table.

I understood what he meant. "No," I admitted.

"We'll be fine, Chels."

****

One month, three weeks and two days ago— Kalamazoo, Michigan

We'd kicked off the "lesser-known tourist destinations of the US" segment with Detroit. It had been a great three days of shooting in the Motor City, and busy ones at that. We'd gone all over to shoot. Henry had dragged us to the Detroit Institute of Art, Hitsville U.S.A., the Fox Theater, and several smaller clubs and venues, not to mention a ton of Greek, Polish, and Middle Eastern restaurants. Between eating, shooting, traveling, and cutting film, I hadn't had a single moment alone with Henry.

All that changed on our last night in Michigan. We were headed to Chicago next, and instead of flying, Henry rented a car and planned to drive. He intended to stop halfway and spend the night at his grandparents' old house, the house where his father had grown up. His grandparents lived in California now, but they'd retained ownership of the house and used it for short-term rentals and as a vacation house for their family. Henry had asked me to join him.

In all our traveling, this was the first time we'd really been on a long car ride. It gave me the chance to truly absorb my surroundings in a way hopping around the world in airplanes couldn't. I got lost watching all the trees, their colors just starting to turn, as they sped by the car window.

When we arrived in Kalamazoo, we'd wandered through town a bit, then Henry had called his dad and gotten a dinner recommendation. After dinner, we drove around with Sean Rush on speakerphone pointing out his childhood haunts, which was a little hard to get used to at first. I mean, how often does one have a famous rock star's iconic voice belting through their car speakers telling you to turn down Drake Street and take a right at the grocery store?

Eventually, we drove to the house, a quaint little Victorian tucked away in a quiet neighborhood. A big, fenced-in yard sat behind it, and a detached garage stood beside it. It was painted butter yellow with white trim and sported an incredible set of gardens.

"My grandmother was a landscape architect," Henry told me as he used the key to open the front door. "It's nice to see the caretaker is keeping up her beloved gardens."

Henry got the door open, flicked a light switch, and then held the door for me. I pulled my backpack up on my shoulder, pushed my glasses to the top of my nose, and walked in.

The house was beautiful, cozy, and quaint, the kind of home anyone might have. It was fully middle-class, well cared for on a budget. It was a far cry from the Morrison mansion I'd grown up in or, I was sure, the house in Malibu Henry had grown up in.

"I love it," I told him honestly as I looked around the living room and open dining room.

"Yeah, it's pretty great." Henry set the keys on an antique table beside the door and moved farther into the house. "Come on, I'll give you the tour." He lifted my backpack off my shoulder and laid it on the couch before taking my hand and pulling me toward the kitchen.

Henry took me through the two stories of the house, stopping to show me the bedrooms where his grandparents, aunt, and uncle had stayed. Then we moved into the finished basement.

"This is it. This is where my dad spent his youth," he said, sweeping his hand across the room.

The room was muted now. Covered in a plush carpet, it contained a dark burgundy couch, coffee table, and a few shelves with books and records. But I could imagine it as the teenage den it had once been. It had probably been filled with concert posters, guitars, and stereo equipment.

"My dad always said he wished we'd had a basement he could give me in my teenage years because he loved this one so much."

I ran my hand over the back of the couch, then

walked around to the front of it and sat down. "Original couch?"

Henry plopped down next to me. "I think so." He ran his hand over the arm. "It's gotta be old as shit."

I laughed. "I'm sure your dad would appreciate that sentiment."

"It's true," he said defensively. "And it's his fault. He's the one who waited until his mid-thirties to have me."

I looked around the brick-walled room. "I bet your dad made out with a bunch of chicks down here."

Henry laughed, throwing his head back. "God. I hadn't ever thought about that. My dad as a randy teenager is pretty hard to picture." He wiped at his eyes. "Yikes."

"Yeah, imagining your parents as beings with sex lives is disturbing. I walked into a room to find my parents making out once. It was pretty awful." I shivered at the memory.

"Once! Shit, that was a regular part of my childhood. My parents were crazy about each other. Still are."

We were quiet for a minute as we both looked around the room that spawned a legendary rock star. Then, suddenly, Henry shifted, moving closer to me. He swung his arm over the back of the couch behind me and placed his mouth a few inches from my ear. "It would have been nice to have a basement of my own so I could seduce girls like you, Chelsea."

I turned my head to look at him. "Please," I said with a snort. "You wouldn't have wasted your time with the likes of me."

"Wanna bet?" he said, just before pulling me into a

kiss.

I didn't resist, not for a second. Instead, I grabbed the back of his head and pulled him closer to me, angling my head and tangling my tongue with his. My glasses went crooked on my face as we pressed together, but neither of us did anything about it.

Just like before, we were both lost in the kiss. Only this time, we were completely sober. Which meant I had a tiny corner of reason left in my brain. So when Henry trailed his hand down my stomach and into my pants, I pulled my head back.

"Wait?" I said. I meant to sound forceful, but instead it came out as a question.

Henry's hand stilled and his brow wrinkled in concern. "You okay?"

"I'm, uh…I'm just wondering if this is a good idea."

"Can't I just give you an orgasm?" he asked, his thumb rubbing gently up and down on my lower abdomen.

"That's *all* you want?" I asked, skepticism in my voice.

"Yep. It's all I want." He smiled at me sweetly, persuasively, like he was asking for a puppy.

"You're weird…ah…oh God." Before I could express how much this baffled me, Henry's hand had traveled down and made its way into my pants. I reached up and popped open the button on my jeans, giving him better access.

"Good girl," Henry whispered, his lips playing at my earlobe.

I leaned my head back on the couch and let my legs go limp in front of me as Henry stroked. Then as my orgasm built up, my muscles all began to tense. My legs went rigid, and my mouth fell open of its own accord.

"That's it, Chels. Let go for me," Henry whispered.

"Oh God!" I cried out as my orgasm crashed into me.

Henry didn't stop his hand, though, and the sensation continued on. "Oh Jesus! Henry! Oh my God! You have to stop."

He did, and my body slumped into the fold of the couch. I sat there for a few minutes just catching my breath. Then I turned to look at him. He had the biggest shit-eating grin on his face.

"Are you sure?" I asked, reaching my hand toward the fly of his jeans.

He caught my hand and pulled it to his lips. He kissed my palm then kept my hand tucked in his. "I'm sure."

"Can we talk about this now?" I asked.

"Sure."

"Why do you think this keeps happening?" I asked him.

For my part, I knew exactly why this kept happening, of course. But I couldn't fathom why Henry was interested in *me*.

"I have a theory about that," he said, leaning against his arm, his face right beside mine.

"Yeah? Let's hear it."

"Well, you and I are close, emotionally and physically. We don't have an ordinary friendship, Chels. I feel as close to you as I do to members of my family. Except you aren't family, so I can still think of you in a sexual way. And we are physically close, you and I." As if to emphasize this he intertwined our fingers. "We work in close proximity, we share a physical presence. And that much closeness..." He shrugged. "It results in...this."

"Hmmm." I was unsure of exactly what to say. It made sense, and it was wholly unromantic. But I it *was* a sensible explanation.

Henry shifted on the couch and pulled me with him so we ended up cuddled up on one end. Then he grabbed the television remote control off the coffee table and flicked the set on. "What should we watch, Chels?"

And just like that, everything went back to normal.

Chapter 12

One month, two weeks ago—Indianapolis, Indiana

"All right," I said, pulling away from Henry's kiss and standing in front of him. "You need to explain this."

Henry leaned back on the small couch in my hotel suite, placing his hands behind his head. His long, jeans-clad legs were spread out in front of him. "Explain what?" he asked, all innocent, like he hadn't just started kissing me while we were watching the latest cut of the show on my laptop.

"Why do you have so much trouble keeping your hands off me when we're alone?" I asked him.

Since the night in Kalamazoo, we hadn't had a moment alone. We were constantly surrounded by the show's crew, or if we weren't, we were with Tom. And here we were alone again, for the first time in days, and we'd instantly started making out again.

"Why is it so hard to comprehend?"

"Because I am *not* hot!" I blurted out. Every time Henry looked at me, I felt like he was looking at an insanely gorgeous showgirl, not a geeky stick figure with four eyes. And the constant speculation as to why was starting to stress me out.

"I vehemently disagree," he said, looking me up and down.

"Seriously?"

"Seriously."

I rested my hand on my hip. "Are you saying you find me irresistibly attractive?"

"Yes." He gave a firm nod. There was no mirth in his eyes or in the set of his mouth.

I narrowed my gaze and scrutinized him. "I thought it was because we're so close, remember."

"Yes. *And* you're insanely hot."

"Am not!"

"Are too!"

I shook my head.

"Wanna make a bet on it?" he challenged.

"What?"

"You get naked for me. And if I am disappointed, you win the bet. If you're as hot as I think you are under those clothes, I win. In fact, I already know what I want if I win. I want to see one of the films you've made."

I stared at him, my mouth agape.

"What do you want if you win, Chels? Not that it matters. Because you won't win."

I finally found my voice. Because I couldn't turn down this opportunity. "If I win, you sing for me."

"Done." He settled farther into the couch. "I'm ready when you are."

"Wait. How do I know you really like what you see? You could easily lie to win the bet."

Without taking his eyes off me, Henry unzipped his fly, exposing the V of his underwear and the outline of the ample, but soft, organ beneath it. "You can see for yourself."

I suddenly realized Henry actually expected me to

strip in front of him. And by taking the bet, I'd agreed.

Crap.

"You can start whenever you'd like," Henry said.

"I'm not doing a strip tease," I said roughly.

"Don't have to. I'm pretty sure you could just throw them off, and it will be hot as hell."

I glanced at the top of his jeans again, then back up at Henry. He watched me, grinning like a fool.

"This is ridiculous," I said, hedging.

"You're not going to back out are you, Chels? I know you well, and I know you don't back away from a challenge, and you're not easily embarrassed. So…"

He was right about both of those things, of course. But they didn't take into account that I stood in front of the one person who I thought was the be-all-end-all of a physical specimen.

I wasn't ashamed of my body. I really did believe in the love-yourself philosophy Candace and I preached to one another on a regular basis. In the past, I'd happily shown my naked form to my sexual partners. And I'd never shied away from this kind of play before.

But stripping in front a man who'd made my blood warm since puberty, a man who was probably used to seeing busty groupies with perfect round asses strut around, a man who was, himself, a gift from the freaking gods…that was a whole different thing.

Nevertheless, I really didn't have a choice that would allow me to save face at this point. "Fine," I said stiffly. I took off my glasses and placed them on the side table. Then I threw off my T-shirt and tossed it on the floor. Without looking at Henry, I pulled off my jeans, taking my socks and panties right along with them. Last, I quickly unclipped my bra and threw it on top of the pile.

Once I was standing there, naked as the day I was born, I looked up at Henry. I started with his face. His eyes were wandering up and down my body, again and again. His lips were parted, and his cheeks were flushed. His body lay in the same relaxed position on the couch, but at the V in his jeans...things had changed, dramatically.

Henry didn't say anything, and I stood there in silence for a couple minutes. Finally, I shifted on my feet and said, "Well. Do I win the bet?"

"Like hell...come here," he said, his voice low and sexy.

I hesitated.

"Please," he begged.

I took the few steps toward him and sat down on his lap, straddling his hips. He pulled my face to his and started kissing me, hard, fast, and desperate. "My God, Chels," he whispered into my mouth.

I pulled my head back a sliver. "Did I lose?"

"You crashed and burned, baby," he said, attacking my neck.

Lost in the sensations Henry was creating, I barely noticed how he shifted our positions until I lay on my back, my naked body pressed against the sofa cushions. Henry kneeled beside the couch, his torso angled so his mouth could make a lovely path over my breasts, down my ribs, across my stomach, his tongue dipping into my bellybutton. And then he kept right on going until my thighs were pressed against his cheeks and I was making sounds I didn't know I was capable of.

I was starting to think Henry must have earned an advanced degree in pleasing women. Unlike every other man who'd been in my bed, Henry could make me come so easily, as if it was second nature to him. And that night, he didn't stop until he'd done it three times.

I could barely move when Henry finally got up from his spot between my legs. He propped my feet up on the arm of the couch and scooted on his knees across the carpet to the other side, where my head propped against the other arm.

"You're trying to kill me," I groaned.

Henry chuckled and kissed me lightly on the lips. "Yes, but it will be a glorious death."

He stood. I got a look at his excitement before he zipped his jeans back up. "I'm gonna go take a shower now, sweetheart. See you in the morning." I watched him walk toward the door. Then he turned and looked back at me again. "Oh, and pick out the best of your films to show me, Chels." After he said this, his gaze lingered on me, lying there, fully satiated and completely naked. "God, you're beautiful." Then, he turned and left.

****

One month, one week, two days ago—Minneapolis, Minnesota

I'd spent the next two days after the incident in Indianapolis feeling guilty. On the orgasm scoreboard, Henry was getting completely ripped off. I realized part of the problem was I had been letting Henry take the lead in all of our encounters. Which was not like me, not at all. In fact, I tended to be the aggressor in my sexual relationships.

When I really analyzed the situation, I decided it was because I'd never been in any kind of sexual situation where I was so unevenly matched with my partner. I'd dated men who were great people, often great in bed, but not the finest physical specimens. Henry's sheer hotness intimidated me. And his desire for me baffled me.

Regardless of why Henry was attracted to me, he was. And, God, I felt like one lucky woman. So, when on our first day of shooting in Minneapolis Henry pulled me into a janitor's closet while everyone else went for lunch, I took over.

I pushed him up against the only wall in the cramped room not covered in shelving and kissed him hard. His hands went to my ass, and he let out a little moan as I straddled one thigh.

"God, Chels. You are freaking amazing," he breathed as I moved my mouth to his neck.

I quickly unbuttoned his jeans and stuck my hand inside. I'd seen the hard length of him beneath a pair of cotton underwear, but actually getting my hands on it made the sheer size so much more real. My mouth spoke before my brain could get control over of it. "Jesus, Henry."

He moaned again and pulled my mouth back to his with one hand behind my head. I pulled his jeans down his thighs, followed by his tight boxer briefs. Henry was huge and hard and downright delicious. Once I had him in my hands, I wanted more. So I dropped to my knees.

"Chels, wait," Henry breathed, placing one hand on my cheek and gently pushing me away from him. "You don't have to do that. I just want to give you a quick orgasm."

"No, Henry. This time, *I'm* going to give *you* an orgasm." I pushed his hand aside and plunged him into my mouth all at once.

"Holy shit!" he cried. "Chels...oh God!"

Henry kept up a litany of moans, groans, and expletives while I played with him. I had no doubt anyone out in the hallway would know exactly what was happening in this closet. When he came, he screamed out my name. I felt like the queen of the freaking world.

****

One month and one week ago—Minneapolis, Minnesota

We were wrapping up the editing on the Midwest episode. Henry, Tom, and I were scrunched around a set of monitors that had been set up on a table in a small conference room at the hotel for us. Steve had been in briefly, told us what he wanted, then left us to do the work.

We collaborated, ignoring Steve's instructions and putting together an incredible show we all felt good about. But throughout the process, as the three of us shared about six square feet of space. Henry and I were constantly coming into physical contact with the brush of a hand, knees rubbing together, forearms sliding past one another. It was a million little touches, and each one made my stomach tighten and my body warm.

By the time we were finally done, I felt like I was on fire. Despite the late hour, Tom suggested we have a celebratory drink. But I couldn't fathom spending any more time in Henry's presence having to behave myself. So I begged off, saying we'd get that drink after we showed the episode to Steve. Tom and Henry agreed, and we all retired separately to our rooms.

I'd only been in my room for about twenty minutes when there was a knock on my door. I'd been about to get in the bath, so I slipped on the fluffy white robe provided by the hotel and went to the door.

I paused for a brief moment, my hand on the doorknob. It was very likely Henry on the other side of the door. I wore only a robe. I was still completely turned on from earlier. It would be wise to tell him to go away or maybe even not open the door at all.

But I opened it, swinging it wide. Henry walked in, shut the door behind him, and pulled me into his arms. I kissed him hard, fast, and deep. Everything I wanted had walked right into my arms.

"Oh my God, you're naked," Henry breathed as he untied the robe and slipped it off me.

I was vaguely aware of a strange rustling noise that couldn't have come from my robe. But it was hard to concentrate as Henry ran his magical hands up and down my body and slid his lips along my neck.

"I was just about to take a bath," I told him breathlessly.

"Hmmm" was his only response.

I heard the rustling again and felt something brush my side. My gaze swept down. A plastic bag swung from Henry's right elbow. The bag was shaped as if it held one relatively small object sitting in the bottom of the bag.

I pulled back so I could concentrate long enough to ask Henry a question. "What's in the bag?"

Henry looked into my eyes as if he were examining me, watching for my reaction as he said, "A box of condoms."

"Thank God," I said, moving back to take his mouth with mine.

Chapter 13

I woke up tangled in Henry's arms. I lay there for a while, listening to his breath, feeling the warmth of his chest against my back.

We'd crossed a line that night, a big fat one. We'd acknowledged it after we'd made love. But we didn't really discuss it. Then we'd stayed in bed watching television for a while before having sex all over again. Henry had spent the night, and I hadn't complained.

But as we'd lain there, both slowly drifting off to sleep, I'd realized everything was at stake. Things were far more tenuous than Henry realized. It wasn't just that our friendship, which was essential to us both, was at risk because of what we'd done. Significantly worse was that I had fallen in love in Henry Rushton.

The panic had bubbled up in me for a moment before I gave in to my exhaustion and the utter relaxation that came from hot sex and comfy cuddling and fell into a deep sleep. Once I woke up, though, I was back to full-blown panic mode.

I had never in my life fallen in love with someone. I'd had a couple of men claim to love me. But I didn't feel the same way, and I'd ended things with them. Those were the men I'd never seen again.

I was absolutely certain I was wholly alone in these feelings. And I had to tread lightly here. I couldn't lose my friendship with Henry over my own inappropriate feelings. I couldn't do that. It would break my heart.

"Hey," he said groggily, placing a kiss on my cheek.

"Hey. I'm starving." I extracted myself from his arms and moved to the side of the bed. "You need to take me to breakfast," I told him as I looked around for my clothes.

"You were just wearing the robe when I came in," Henry said, guessing what I was after.

I spotted the robe on the floor over by the door. "Oh yeah. Well, I'm going to shower," I said casually. "Be back here in twenty minutes to take me to breakfast."

Without looking at him, I walked into the bathroom and leaned over, my hands planted on the sink. I gazed into the mirror. I looked like I'd just had sex with my best friend, twice. My hair was crazy mussed up, the curls flying everywhere. My eyes were bright, and my lips looked a little swollen.

"What the hell did you do?" I asked myself.

I could hear Henry moving around in the next room, so I turned the water on in the shower. Like all the others, this was a pretty nice hotel and rather than a tub/shower combo, this bathroom had both a Jacuzzi tub and a stand-up shower. I glanced briefly at the still full bathtub I'd abandoned last night before pulling the tub's drain and walking into the shower. I shut the opaque glass door behind me just as the bathroom door opened. My skin jumped.

"Henry?" I called.

He didn't answer, instead he opened the shower door and walked right in.

"What are you doing?" I asked while

simultaneously looking him up and down. I couldn't help it. Naked Henry was the most beautiful thing I'd ever seen.

"Taking a shower so I can take you to breakfast," he said, fully stealing my water.

He stood under the showerhead. The water cascaded down his long hair and over his strong shoulders. Streams of clear liquid poured over the muscles of his chest and lower, to his six-pack, and lower still. My gaze followed its flow.

"Are you cold?" he asked.

My head snapped up. He was watching me, his brow scrunched up.

"Huh?"

"You're shivering, Chels." He took me by the shoulders and turned us so I was under the hot water and he stood where I'd just been. "Skinny girls," he said, shaking his head.

"Whatever. We can't all be covered in muscle."

He snorted and grabbed the shampoo. He poured an ample amount into his palm then stuck the bottle on the shelf behind him.

"Hey, maybe I need some," I complained.

"This *is* for you. Turn around."

Like all women, I'd dreamed of the day I would meet a man who voluntarily washed my hair without being asked. It was right up there with a man who liked to give oral sex. Apparently, in Henry, I'd found both.

With a deeply satisfied sigh, I turned my back to him. I heard him lather the shampoo in his hands, then he started to work it into my hair. And it really was everything I wanted it to be.

I let out a little moan, which prompted Henry to

pull me to his chest. "Jesus, Chels. I love your sounds." His soapy hands moved out of my hair and down over my breasts.

"We really have to talk, Henry," I said slowly, still languishing in the sensations he was causing.

"We will, Chels, over breakfast," he whispered in my ear. "But first…" He turned me around so I faced him, and he started to kiss me.

I knew I should have resisted. We needed to talk, badly. And continuing down this path without so much as a decent conversation about it was not going to help. But I couldn't seem to muster the will. So when Henry pushed me up against the wall and cupped my ass, I wrapped my legs around his waist.

Henry whispered in my ear. "Don't move. We have to make it the bedroom where the condoms are."

I stayed wrapped around him like a spider monkey as he shoved the faucet knob down before securing me in his arms and walking us both into the other room. Still dripping wet, we collapsed on the bed, our mouths fused together in a searing kiss.

Henry pulled away from me long enough to search for a condom on the bedside table. I used the opportunity to kiss his neck, still slick with warm water. Once he had the thing out of its package, he rolled over so I was on top of him.

I plucked the condom from his hand and sat up on my knees, straddling his thighs. I grinned as I rolled the condom down over him. Then I stroked him from the base to the head, squeezing just a bit. Henry's head wrenched back, his eyes closed. A moan escaped from his throat, vibrating his neck which now stretched in front of me.

I felt a heady sense of power over this magnificent creature. "You want more?" I asked, my voice low and seductive.

Henry's head moved forward and his eyelids fluttered open, revealing those melting chocolate irises that matched the mischief in my own. "You want me to beg?"

"No need," I said as I moved so that I settled myself on him. In one quick and monumental movement, he was inside me again.

It was just as much of a life-affirming act as it had been the first time Henry had slowly inched into me from above, perhaps even better. Gone was Henry's careful concern and his intense, and unnecessary, restraint as he hovered over me. Now we were as we should be, two people who wanted each other and felt no inhibitions about needing it.

Gone too, was any need to be quiet or reserved. As I moved deftly on top of him, we both made noise. I called out his name, and he moaned mine. We thanked higher deities and spewed obscenities. And after we'd both come, shaking and keening together, we pulled each other into a tight cuddle, unable to do anything but breathe deeply and be grateful for what we'd stumbled into.

****

"Okay, this is serious. We *have* to sort this out."

It had taken us another hour to actually get clean and dressed. Then we'd taken a cab to a restaurant a few miles away so we didn't run the risk of bumping into someone from the show. Thankfully, we still had a couple of hours before we had to meet up with everyone else at the airport.

I had no idea how painful this conversation was going to be, but we simply *had* to have it.

"Look, Chels. I think you're overreacting. I don't think it's a big deal. You said yourself you've had this arrangement before," Henry said, preempting the conversation as soon as we'd ordered our breakfast.

"And I told you it had a fifty-fifty success rate. I also told you it wasn't the same as *us*," I said, pointing between the two of us.

Henry took my hand and held it on the table. "You're upset."

"I'm not upset," I protested. "I'm worried."

"Okay. What do I need to do to make you not worry?" He leaned toward me, his deep brown eyes settling on my own.

I took a long breath, trying to be as calm about all of this as Henry. "We need to set some ground rules."

He took a sip of his coffee and leaned back in his chair. "Okay. Anything you want."

I sat straight in my chair and ticked off the rules on my fingers. "Number one, as soon as one of us is interested in someone else romantically, we have to say so." I knew it would be Henry, not me, who would be the one saying he'd found someone else. I was in way too deep. But that was part of the reason for these rules. I would need time to adjust when he found someone else. I couldn't have it be a surprise. "Like, as soon as you feel like asking someone out, not after you've asked them out," I said, to emphasize how serious I was about this.

"Okay."

"Number two is, when we cut it off, we do it just like that." I snapped my fingers with my free hand. "No lingering. We *immediately* go back to being just friends, no benefits." My chest tightened at the thought of losing out on what I'd had last night and this morning.

Henry's gaze pierced mine and his brow bunched up. I was glad to see he was taking this seriously. "Okay."

"Number three."

"How long is this list?"

"Last one. Number three is that it has to be a secret. As far as the rest of the world knows, we're just friends. And that goes for *everyone*."

"Even Tom?"

I nodded. "I won't even tell my brother. No one. It'll be easier this way. We won't have to answer any questions or live up to any bizarre expectations."

"Bizarre expectations?" he asked, cocking his head.

"Yeah, when Gary and I were…doing this, we told some people close to us or they knew anyway. And they all expected us to start dating. They didn't understand when we didn't. And a few of them really flipped out when he started dating someone else. They acted affronted, like he was betraying me, or they were sad and sorry for me, like we'd broken up. It was just ridiculous. I don't want to have to deal with it."

"Okay, it's our secret," Henry agreed. "Is that it?"

"Yes. That's it. I think…I think we can retain our friendship this way."

"Don't *think*, Chels," Henry said, a very serious look on his face. "Our friendship is very important to me. We *will* keep it intact."

I nodded, swallowing hard. I wasn't so sure this would work. After all, I'd already made a huge mistake by falling for Henry.

****

One month ago—Kansas City, Missouri

I hedged. "I just finished it. I sent it to Jack yesterday. He hasn't watched it yet, so...I don't know if it's any good." I stood in front of the screen, not really wanting to move and show my film to Henry.

He grinned. "So, does that mean I will be the first one to see it?"

I bit my lip and nodded.

"Not even Tom has seen it?"

I shook my head.

His grin grew wider, and he settled deeper into the couch. Then, he patted the seat beside him gently. "Let's get started, Chels."

I lingered in front of the television for a moment longer. I had, in fact, lost the bet. Henry was certainly turned on by my strip tease (which had been sadly without any tease). There was no denying it. So now I had to pay my debt. And I was nervous as hell about it.

"Come on, afterward we'll go get Kansas City burnt ends at the barbecue place across the street," he promised. "Come on, Chels."

I sighed heavily. I hit the play button then quickly skipped to the couch, plopping down harshly beside Henry. He pulled me against his chest and tucked his arms around me.

We watched my film in complete silence. I'd made the documentary for Jack's nonprofit. It addressed the issue of homelessness. It was relatively short, but I remained completely tense for the entire twenty-six minutes. When the film ended and the screen went black, I turned to Henry, my muscles like tight rubber bands, my eyes meeting his tentatively.

"You are so talented, Chels," he said softly, his dark eyes dancing. "I mean, that was…it was so amazing!"

"Thanks," I said quietly, pulling my gaze away from his.

"You have a bright future with this, Chels."

I shrugged. "I did it for free for my brother, Jack. It's not exactly—"

"It's just the beginning," he said, squeezing my shoulders.

"You really liked it?"

"Hell, yes." Henry pulled one arm away from my shoulder and placed his palm on my cheek. "Look, I get why you're insecure about this. I feel the same way about my writing. But I'm completely serious about this. You are very, very good."

My muscles started to loosen, and I felt myself relax under his touch. "You gonna let me read something you wrote?" I asked, hoping he would reciprocate in this game of sharing.

"Sure. I have a short story I'll put on your e-reader tomorrow, okay?"

I nodded, suppressing the giant grin that threatened to make an appearance as I anticipated getting to read something Henry had written.

Henry put his arms back around me, and I nuzzled farther into his chest. He kissed the top of my head. "So, tell me how you see your future."

"Hmmm. Well, I'm going to do fewer gigs over the next couple of years. I want to spend more time filming for my own projects. I also need to spend time talking to investors and engaging stations to air my work, stuff like that. I'm hoping that within five years, I'll have at least one full-length film produced and sold. After that"—I shrugged—"sky's the limit." I turned my body a little so I could see his face better. "What about you, Henry?"

He pushed a strand of hair off my cheek and tucked it behind my ear, then he fiddled with the arm of my glasses. "I haven't really planned it out. I guess I've just been focused on selling one story at a time."

"Come on," I coaxed. "You must have given it *some* thought. Where do you see yourself in five years?"

He laughed. "What is this? A job interview?"

I stuck my tongue out at him.

"I don't know. Hopefully, financially stable. Or maybe married to a woman with a good career so I can stay home and be a failed writer."

"So, you're going to find a woman who's gonna carry your ass?" I teased.

"Hey, I'll take care of the kids."

I sat up and looked intently at him. "Are you serious? About wanting the wife and kids, I mean." I was shocked, though I couldn't name why.

"Sure. Why not?" he said, looking completely innocent.

"I...I don't know. It isn't something I've ever really given any thought to. And I guess I'm always a little surprised when someone my age has it all figured out."

"You never thought about it?"

I shrugged. "Not really, no."

"I have," he said, tucking me back into his side. "But my chances of getting a happily-ever-after are slim."

"Why's that?" I asked, my mind still reeling as I tried to keep up with this head-spinning conversation.

"My parents."

"What did they do?" I asked, confused.

He chuckled and the movement of his chest vibrated beneath me in a delicious way. "They set my expectations too high."

"How so?"

"If you ever saw them together, it wouldn't require an explanation. But they are insanely in love, even after all these years. It's tangible in the air around them. Even when they fight, you can see it all over them. And having grown up with them as my example, I don't think I could ever make a lifelong commitment with anything less than that all-consuming love. So…it may never happen."

Silence sat between us for a long time. My mind was whirring with questions. Who would be the woman that finally got into Henry's heart? Would I like her? Would she be someone I'd know, be friends with?

To disguise my internal turmoil, I said flippantly, "Fucking pessimist."

****

Three weeks ago—Denver, Colorado

"They freaking love it!" Steve slammed a purplish folder down on the table in front of him. "We have the highest-rated show on the network right now, people."

Steve had continued his pouty, martyred attitude toward the show right up until tonight. He'd allowed Henry, Tom, and me to completely take over our portion of the show, and he'd only half-assed the other part. But now he was more than willing to take credit for the show's success.

"He better not start trying to micromanage us," Tom whispered from beside me.

Steve opened the folder and fiddled with some papers inside. "I've got some audience feedback we need to keep in mind as we wrap up the season with the last few shows. We want to end on the highest note possible and set up for a killer second season."

I watched as Henry sat back in his chair and crossed his arms over his chest. He sat directly across the large oval conference table from me, but his gaze was fixed on a spot on the polished oak in front of him.

"Okay, they love watching Tyressa go to the nightclubs. Especially the men. They say you're a great dancer, sweetie."

Tyressa beamed.

"And the women think Henry is sexy as hell."

Henry rolled his eyes.

"In fact, the whole going out to museums and shit seems to make you seem even sexier," Steve said, looking over at Henry, who grimaced. "So, nice suggestion."

"It was Chelsea's idea," Henry said, snapping his head up.

"Nicely done," Steve said, actually bothering to look at me as he said it. "And I gotta say, we're gonna have a winner with this 'taking your mom to the history museum' thing."

"It isn't a 'thing,' " Henry protested. "I am going to hang out with my mom. I didn't invite any cameras along."

I knew he was cranky about this, even though his mom had agreed to it. His hesitation had finally given way last week after much harassment by Steve. But now, he regretted it.

Steve ignored this. "We asked some of the women surveyed, and they lost their shit over the idea. Universally, they thought it was like the hottest thing they'd ever freaking heard of." Steve shrugged. "Women are weird."

Henry sighed and went back to staring at the table.

"So, we do the museum tomorrow, and other than that, you got this stop off as requested, Henry." After saying that, Steve turned to Tyressa and her team. He explained what they needed to do during their Denver shooting.

When Steve released us fifteen minutes later, Henry bolted out of the little conference room and headed straight for the elevator. I caught up with him as he hit the down button.

"You headed to the airport to pick up your mom?" I asked.

"Yeah, you wanna come?"

"No. Thanks, but I have some work to do this afternoon."

"But we'll see you for dinner?" he asked, raising one eyebrow as if he were challenging me to back out.

"Um, how about after dinner? We could go out for drinks or something," I suggested.

"Okay, but don't flake." He pointed his finger at me, a deep crease marring his perfectly proportionate forehead. "My mom is dying to meet you, and I don't want the first time to be while we're shooting tomorrow."

Henry had asked to break my rules. He'd said there was no way his mom wouldn't figure out what was going on with us. And I'd agreed, partly because I'd already accidently outed our arrangement to Tom. But, of course, this made me even more nervous about meeting her.

But I didn't let that show as I said, "Don't worry. I'll be there."

Chapter 14

I stood in front of the hotel room, nervous as hell. I'd been pacing in the hallway for a good ten minutes, and I knew I had to just stop and make myself knock on the door.

When I'd first arrived, I'd told myself I had no idea why I was nervous about meeting Henry's mom. But over the course of my obsessive pacing, I'd admitted to myself it was because I was afraid she'd see right through me.

Before I could worry myself further over this terrifying thought, I knocked on the door. Thirty seconds later, the door swung open, and I got my first in-person look at Dani "Baby" Rush.

"Chelsea!" she shouted, pulling me into the room and throwing her arms around me. When she pulled me back to arm's length and said, "Let me look at you!" I took my chance to examine her, too.

She was around my height. She didn't look anywhere near old enough to have a twenty-six-year-old son, and she was way too ordinary-looking to have had her picture in magazines.

She was pretty, for sure, but not glamorous, not at all. She had long, straight hair that was a plain brown color streaked with a little gray. Her otherwise smooth face held distinct laugh lines around her bright blue eyes. And there was a just a hint of Henry there in her face, the nose perhaps, and the long eyelashes.

"I have been dying to meet you," she told me.

"Me too, Mrs…" What the hell was I suppose to call her? My brain rooted around frantically. Her real name was Danielle Rushton, but all the papers called her Baby Rush. I couldn't imagine calling this woman "Baby," but then, did I use Mrs. Rush or Mrs. Rushton?

Fortunately, she helped me out. "Call me Baby…No wait. You know what? Call me Dani."

"Okay, Dani."

She smiled. "Wow. That feels nice. No one other than my sister has called me Dani in years. Even my parents call me Baby." She rolled her eyes, and right there I could see her in Henry.

She seemed to be ruminating internally about her name, so I took a moment to look around the substantial hotel suite to locate Henry. The suite had two doors off the main room. I happened to know from having spent the night before in this very suite that one was a bathroom and the other was a separate bedroom. I assumed Henry was in one of them.

"God, we have so much to talk about," Dani said as she ushered me over to the couch. A bottle of wine sat on the coffee table, and she poured two glasses. Then, as I sat down, she handed me one and sat beside me. "Red okay?"

"Sure." I wiggled out of my jacket and let it fall behind me before taking the glass and indulging in a long drink. "Um, isn't Henry having any?" I asked, looking at the two glasses, one in my hand and one in hers.

"He's not here." She settled back in the couch, angling toward me. "Right after we got back from dinner I got a call from the airline saying they located my suitcase. I never usually check my bags. I always just take carry-on. But practically every member of my damn family sent me something to bring Henry. And most of it was food, including a jar of homemade preserves from his Uncle Mike. So I had to check a bag for the first time in, like, twenty years, and of course, it got lost. Anyway, he went to the airport to go get it, and I stayed here in case you showed up. He should be back in fifteen or twenty minutes."

I was floored. How could Henry not have warned me I would be alone with his mom? "Oh...um...I'm surprised he didn't text me," I said quietly.

She laughed. "He left his phone here. He was a little frazzled today. It was kind of weird, to be honest with you. I mean, I'm not the kind of mom who makes her son nervous when she visits. In fact, I think I'm pretty damn chill. I asked him what was up, but he wouldn't tell me."

"Huh?" I said. "I don't know. He seemed fine this afternoon when I saw him. Except that..." I grinned, remembering Henry's reaction to Steve's declaration that women found him hot.

Dani sat up a little, looking very much like she wanted to be in on the secret. "Yes?"

I told her about the meeting, especially the part where Steve talked about the women wanting Henry, and I described Henry's reaction. "He sat there and rolled his eyes," I told her.

"You know, I think Henry's aversion to women who are attracted to him is pretty crippling, so I hate to say this, but I find it to be hilarious. You'd think he was being tortured when a beautiful girl hits on him." She laughed. "His dad likes to tease him about it. He calls it 'Henry's burden.' "

"It is truly ridiculous," I told her, smiling. I liked this woman, a lot. Within moments, she'd made me feel comfortable in her presence, and I sensed a kinship with her. We were both women who had an understanding of Henry he himself didn't even see. And we both loved him.

That thought had my entire body tensing. I stiffened my spine and squeezed the wine glass in my hand. It was as if I was convinced she could read my mind. Just having thought it in her presence had me panicked. Which was, of course, ridiculous, especially since I thought it in front of Henry all the time and it didn't cause any panic.

Dani sipped her wine and examined me. I sat there, avoiding her gaze and feeling like I was waiting to be tortured. "Chelsea?"

"Hmmm?"

"What's going on between you and Henry?"

My eyes darted to her. "What...what do you mean?"

She set her wine glass down on the coffee table and leaned toward me. "I mean, Henry has a tough time having relationships with women he isn't related to. And you and he are close. You have a strong friendship, and you're sleeping together." My face must have showed my discomfort when she brought this up because she laughed and put her hand over mine. "You look about as scared as Henry did when he told me, in what was a hilarious and convoluted conversation, I might add. What? You think I was a virgin until my wedding night?" She rolled her eyes.

I laughed and relaxed a little. "I suppose not."

"You suppose correctly. Anyway, what I don't get is why you two are claiming to be 'just friends.' What is that all about?"

"This is precisely why we have been keeping this a secret. Because people don't understand. I told my friend Tom, too, and he said the same thing."

"Hmmm...so why?"

I was nervous all over again. Somehow this short conversation had me on an emotional rollercoaster. I shrugged. "We're just friends."

"Bullshit."

Torn between amusement, shock, and frustration at her statement, what came out was tears. I felt the quiet sob rise in my chest, and before I could stop it, it erupted from my throat, followed by one hot tear trickling out of my left eye and dripping down my cheek.

Dani moved closer and put an arm around my shoulders. "Shit. My son is being an ass, isn't he?"

I shook my head. I wanted to defend Henry, but I couldn't speak just then.

"Are you in love with him, Chelsea?" she asked softly.

Before I could think about it, before I could realize she'd just asked the one question I'd spent hours being terrified she would ask, before I could come up with a lie, I nodded.

"Let's get out of here," she said, standing and pulling me up with her.

I swiped at my cheeks with my palms and stared at her. "What?"

"I know a place," Dani said, walking over to the

counter by the small kitchenette. She grabbed a small square notepad and scribbled something quickly on it.

I threw my jacket back on and took a few steps forward to peer over her shoulder. She'd left a simple note to Henry saying we'd gone out and we'd be back later. Then she grabbed her big, brown mom purse and pulled me from the room.

Chapter 15

Present day—Los Angeles, California
Henry

I run my hand through my hair and lean back in the uncomfortable couch. "So I get back from the airport and they're gone." I've just finished telling the story, up to the point where my mom and Chelsea took off on me, and I can feel the tale taking a dark turn. I'm exhausted at the prospect of explaining the rest of it.

"Hmmm," my father says. He's sitting across from me in a metal folding chair, one leg crossed over his knee, his hands resting on his thighs. He's looking at me like he's examining me to make sure I'm in one piece. His eyebrows are scrunched up. Below them, his eyes are narrowed.

Suddenly, it occurs to me he might know something. I sit up and lean toward him. "Did Mom tell you what she and Chelsea talked about that night?"

"Hmmm. Some."

"Dad, you gotta tell me." He doesn't respond. "I know you're going to give me some line about how you can't give away confidences," I argue. "But this is *my life*. I mean—"

My dad holds his hand, palm out, in front of his face. This is a sign I recognize. In my family, my dad is, without a doubt, the quiet one. His words are rare and heavily weighted. So the rest of us just keep talking until he responds. But he won't ever interrupt, and if he doesn't get the chance you may miss what he was going to say altogether. So, he's developed this habit of holding up his hand when he has something to say.

I nod, indicating he should go ahead. My dad says, "I'll tell you what your mom told me. But first I want to hear what she told *you*."

I glance at the clock because this conversation is getting long. My dad knows what I'm thinking and waves his hand at me. "We have time."

I subconsciously glance at the door. "What about Billy?"

"Like you care," he says.

He's right. I don't care. Billy is the replacement camera operator Trek assigned to me when Chelsea didn't show up in LA. And tonight, I am supposed to be shooting my very last scenes for the show. I'm at a concert my dad and Uncle Hank are performing in town. My dad had showed up early to shoot some B-roll scenes of us hanging out before he had to go on stage. But as soon as he'd seen me, he knew something was up.

So, we'd ditched Billy with my uncle and disappeared into my dad's green room. We've been in here for a while now while I explained about Chelsea and me.

I'd been doing all the talking, and now I want his advice. I feel like I am stuck in the worse situation of my life, or at least the most painful. But I know I have to give him what he wants first.

"Mom came back late. I'd been waiting up for her. She thought that was funny as hell. She told me she and

Chelsea had gone to some bar she knew about across town and hung out. I tried to get her to tell me what they'd talked about. But she stayed tightlipped. She went to bed. And, Dad, I couldn't sleep worth a shit."

My dad grins. I continue with the story. "So the next morning, before we went to the museum to meet up with Chelsea, I took Mom to breakfast. I demanded she tell me what she and Chelsea talked about. She said they were friends now. She said Chelsea was a beautiful, intelligent, charming woman, and she thought the world of her. And I said, 'I know all that, Mom.' And then you know what she did? She smacked me on the forehead and told me 'Wake up.' " I demonstrate by slamming my palm into my own head, much the way my mother had that day.

My dad laughs.

"Then we get to the museum, and she and Chelsea fall into each other's arms. Literally, Dad. They're, like, best friends overnight. And they talk and giggle and all that shit. And neither of them will give me the time of day while we're all together. The next day, I take Mom to the airport and just before she gets ready to go through security, I asked her one more time to tell me what she and Chelsea talked about. She said, 'I love you, Henry. But I can't help you with this.' Then she kissed my cheek and walked away. It was so frustrating!"

"I bet."

"Come on, Dad. Tell me what Mom told you."

As he's prone to do, my dad takes a long pause. I watch impatiently as he takes a few deep breaths, rubs his chin with his thumb and forefinger, and shifts slightly in his chair, all the while staring intently at me.

Finally, he says, "Your mom told me Chelsea confessed to her she's in love in with you."

"Shit," I say, leaning my head back. Then I admit what I already knew deep down. "I kinda figured."

"Listen, Buddy, here's what I don't get. How the *fuck* did you not figure this shit out sooner?" Now he's looking at me with a sense of sheer confusion. And I can understand why. But I feel defensive.

"We were just *friends*, Dad. And we had rules. Rules Chelsea set by the way."

"So you were just friends having sex, right?"

"Yes," I say, finally feeling like maybe someone understands.

"And you didn't think there was anything more to it? I mean, come on." He tosses his hands a few inches into the air in front of him in a muted expression of disbelief. It is highly uncharacteristic for my dad.

I throw my own hands up in the air in a much more exaggerated version of his gesture. "Why would there be? We were *friends*, and we were just having sex, Dad!" I say, my frustration resurfacing.

I'm getting worked up, but he goes right back to his usual calm and relaxed state. He leans farther back in his chair and folds his arms over his chest. "I was friends with your mom once, too, and then we started having sex."

I bury my head in my hands. "First of all, gross. Secondly, what on earth does that have to do with anything?"

"We're much more than friends now."

My father's words are hitting me a hell of a lot harder than I am willing to admit to myself, let alone to him. So, I stay quiet. I listen to the chair creak beneath him as he shifts. I listen to my own heartbeat as it tortures me.

"Okay, Henry," he says softly. "Why don't you tell me how you ended up here, looking miserable as shit."

"I thought I had it good, Dad. I really did. Then everything started to go to hell. And it was entirely my fault." I lean back and tell my dad the rest of the story.

****

Two weeks, four days ago—Jackson Hole, Wyoming

I had trouble focusing on the shoot that afternoon. The scenery was gorgeous and completely distracting. Surrounded by the majesty of the "North American Alps," the jagged peaks of the Grand Teton range looked as though they were ripped out of the earth like pages in a book and set on end, scraping the bright blue sky, and inspiring neck-craning awe.

On top of that, the unseasonably warm day had brought out the sexy in Chelsea's wardrobe. October in Wyoming should have seen her bundled up in a coat, hat and mittens. Instead, it was nearly sixty degrees and sunny so she wore a flouncy cotton skirt that landed well above her knees with a pair of gray tights. It was paired with a not-so-loose tank top and a fitted fleece that was happily unzipped. Her hair was pushed up in a perfectly messy bun at the back of her head, and she spent the vast majority of the day pushing her glasses up on her nose with one finger.

I wanted to whisk her off into the woods on the other side of the yawning lake and fool around like teenagers who'd escaped their parents' sight on a camping trip. But I was doubtful that would happen. Chelsea hadn't so much as given me a peck on the cheek since Denver. I also hadn't gotten a word out of her about what she'd discussed with my mom.

"Henry, I think this is what we'll open the show with," Chelsea said, referring to the short introductory speech I'd just made on camera while standing at the Jenny Lake overlook. "Now I want to shoot some B-roll of you walking down the trail that leads away from the viewpoint and around the lake."

She turned to the park ranger, who acted as our guide. He just nodded. The Park Service required all media to have an escort, and Kevin was supposed to be monitoring us as we filmed in the park. He was an old friend of my mom's. He'd worked with her a million years ago when she was a seasonal park ranger at Yellowstone. Now near retirement, he was pretty relaxed and laid back, letting us do whatever we'd like.

I stood at the edge of the trail, near the crowded viewpoint, feeling extremely awkward. There were at least thirty people here, all staring directly at me. And they'd been doing exactly that since we first started filming here nearly an hour ago. I'd managed to block them all out and get the shot done, but I was grateful for the suggestion we move into a more remote location.

I grabbed the heaviest of Chelsea's equipment bags and took the lead down the pathway. The narrow trail forced us to walk single file. This configuration did not allow for followers and with the addition of Tom's gruff statements to the looky-loos, we managed to lose everyone.

I scouted out a place to stop for the shot Chelsea wanted. I chose a spot where the dirt and rock path widened out beneath the skinny trunks of the lodgepole pines, which were peppered with thicker firs and spruces. Peeking out behind the trees were splashes of bright blue from the picturesque lake. I was happy with the scenery there and, perhaps more important, the solitude the location provided. So I stopped and turned to Chelsea and Tom.

"Perfect," Chelsea said, unfolding the tripod.

Tom looked around briefly, then nodded in agreement.

"Good. Let me know when you're ready," I said, folding my arms over my chest and leaning up against the nearest tree.

Chelsea set up her equipment, aiming the camera down the trail so she could take footage of me walking away from and back toward it. Tom fiddled with more equipment a few yards away, and Kevin stood about fifty feet away, also resting against a tree, his head thrown back, his hat over his eyes like he was sleeping or something.

"So, Chels. You talk to my mom since Denver?" I asked, trying to sound casual.

She didn't look at me, her gaze was still focused on the equipment in front of her as she harrumphed. "Wouldn't you like to know?"

"This is getting a little ridiculous," I complained. "Just tell me about your conversation."

She laughed out loud this time.

"What's the matter, Henry? Worried they're keeping secrets from you?" Tom asked, looking up at me with a smirk on his face. I frowned at him, but he just grinned at me and chuckled.

"Maybe I am."

"Why don't you ask your mom about it?" Chelsea suggested while peering through the eye of the camera.

I let out a heavy sigh. This wasn't getting me

anywhere. I knew I would have to try a different tactic. But subtlety just wasn't my thing.

I stayed quiet until eventually Chelsea asked me to walk down the trail. I approached her so we were just inches away from each other and whispered, "Tit for tat. I'll get you your shot if you promise to give me one little detail about your conversation with my mom."

She rolled her eyes. "Fine. Whatever. You first."

I wasn't good at blackmail, or at negotiating with women. Hell, I was terrible at it. They were all far more cunning than me, not to mention smarter. And all my life, the women in my family had managed to manipulate me and bend me to their will.

This attempt was probably going to backfire. But I tried it anyway. I obediently followed Chelsea's directions, walking back and forth on the trail while Tom and Kevin sat silently by.

When we were finished shooting and all packed up, I walked down the trail just behind Chelsea. We were in the rear, so when I pressed her to tell me a detail as she'd promised, and she stopped on the trail and turned to face me, we fell even farther behind the two men.

Chelsea hefted the bag she carried on her shoulder and pushed her glasses up with her free hand. "Okay, you want a detail?"

"Yeah."

"What kind of detail?" she asked, one eyebrow raised provocatively.

"I don't know," I shrugged. "Something…something important."

"Important? What does that mean?"

I racked my brains for how to answer this in a way that would get me what I wanted. "Um…something about…"

"Yes?" she challenged.

"Sex. Something about sex," I blurted out, feeling like an awkward teenager all of a sudden.

"Okay." She grinned. And I should have known right there I was in trouble. "We had a long and detailed conversation about the most interesting places we've ever had sex. I mean, honestly, I thought I was pretty adventurous. After all, the janitor's closet didn't even rate on my list. But your parents put me to shame. Did you know they once got it on at—"

"Ugh! Stop!" I covered my ears with my hands.

Chelsea laughed heartily. Then she turned around and started walking back down the trail.

"Wait!" I called, jogging to keep up. "That's it?"

"I gave you a detail," she called over her shoulder.

Damn it. I'd lost again.

****

Two weeks ago—Bozeman, Montana

Tom's back was to us as he opened the door and walked through it. Then his image, distorted through the thick glass, curved toward the tan-colored minivan we were renting. He angrily brushed the dusting of snow off the windshield and hopped in the driver's seat. A moment later, he was gone.

I let out my breath and turned to Chelsea. She'd been just as intently focused on Tom as I had been. She ripped her gaze away from the front door and looked around the lobby. It wasn't really bustling; there were maybe a dozen people in here, mostly families. But it was relatively quiet, which is why, after consultation with the staff, we'd chosen this time of day to film at the popular Museum of the Rockies.

"Let's catch the planetarium show," Chelsea suggested, pointing toward the kiosk over the front desk. It announced a show about exo-planets.

I looked at the clock on my phone. It was going to take Tom at least thirty minutes to drive back to the hotel, retrieve the spare battery we needed, and drive back to us. "Sure," I agreed, placing my hand on the small of Chelsea's back. It was a simple movement, one designed to indicate I was following her toward our shared goal. I must have done it a million times in the past. But this time, she stiffened. I pulled my hand away and repressed a sigh.

I reached down to help carry her gear, since she was still clutching the coat that had become her lifeline when winter had arrived in Montana the day before in the form of a light snow and freezing cold wind. She let me carry all but one small bag, which was a novelty lately since she'd been increasingly stubborn about hauling her own stuff.

I followed her, a couple steps behind, into the dark theater. We piled the stuff against one wall and settled into chairs near the rear. We both immediately leaned back in the seats as they were designed to encourage. Both of our eyes focused on the blank screen above us.

"What should we have for dinner for tonight?" I asked.

"I don't know. Maybe I'll just order a salad from room service...I have some things to work on."

I shifted in my seat so I could look at Chelsea. She kept her gaze overhead. With a view of her from the side, I admired her profile. She had a soft nose, regal chin, and the most perfect cheeks I'd ever seen. She was absolutely beautiful. "Oh yeah? What are you working on?"

She shrugged. "Just a little something."

"Like?"

She still didn't look at me as she answered. "I have an idea for a short. I'm drawing out some storyboards. But…um…I'll have to wait until I get home to really get started."

"Oh yeah? Why?"

She shrugged again. "I need some help with the dialogue."

"You need a writer," I suggested.

She let out her breath. "Yes."

"Well, you're in luck. I'm a writer. And I happen to be free."

"We'll see," was her lukewarm response.

I felt hurt and awkward. So, I turned back in my seat, head facing up, mirroring Chelsea's position. We sat there in a deep silence for the next four minutes until the stupid show finally started. As the stars moved across the dome above me and a soothing voice blanketed us from the speakers at the edge of the room, my mind wandered.

I remembered, in vivid detail, a bright, sunny day in Des Moines, Iowa. We had walked through the sculpture park hand in hand. We'd moved slowly along the path through massive pieces of artwork. It had been a true mosey. Young families had passed us with kids who were just learning to walk. But we'd continued on our slow and peaceful stroll.

We'd talked the entire way. I remembered the amused smile on Chelsea's face as I'd described the tour I'd accompanied my dad on at the age of fifteen. My awakening to the world as it really was, as well as my father's fumbling attempts to soften my realizations, had provided her with ample entertainment.

I remembered she had told me a long story about a family vacation from her childhood. Her descriptions were acute and ripe with easily visualized mementos. Her ability to weave a story, using my own imagination as a tool, never failed to impress me.

Afterward, we'd eaten dinner at a twenty-four-hour breakfast place, then walked three miles through the city back to our hotel. We'd walked into her room and fallen on one another.

I remembered clearly the prolonged foreplay that night. We must have fooled around for nearly two hours before finally taking ourselves out of that wonderful moment of anticipation and sinking into one another.

I remembered feeling that night like I was closer to Chelsea than I'd ever been to anyone else in the world. I looked over at her in the darkened planetarium. Her face was stiff and distant, her eyes locked on the screen above her, and away from me. How had we gotten here?

Chapter 16

One week, three days ago—Seattle, Washington

I needed alone time with Chelsea, desperately. So, I'd casually suggested Chelsea take the night off from editing. But I'd done it in front of Tom. And that was the key because he'd joined in, and the two of us were able to bully her into it.

Then, I took her out to dinner at a dimly-lit Italian restaurant. We sat in a cozy booth, side by side, rather than across from one another, sipping wine and dwelling over appetizers when I reached under the table and gently stroked her knee.

Our conversation had been going well up until then. In fact, it had been going a lot better than our halted discussions of late. So I knew I was taking a big risk by turning things sexual. But Chelsea didn't pause in her story. She just smiled and continued to tell me about Jack and Candace's epic fight over whether or not they should enroll their puppy in "doggy daycare."

I kept my hand there and slowly caressed her through her jeans. Then I moved my hand up. Over the course of the meal and our long, lazy conversation, I managed to move my hand all the up to the juncture of her thighs. And over dessert, my fingers got downright wicked.

Despite the barrier of her jeans between us, I could

tell I was affecting her. Her eyes drooped, and she bit her lip, staring at me, hard. Her breathing was heavy.

"You wanna go?" I asked her, picking up the check and reluctantly moving my hand away from her.

She nodded.

We ran through the rain and into the arms of a waiting cab. Once we were nestled into the back, I pulled her across the leather seat so her thigh was pressed up against mine and put my hand under her blouse, allowing my thumb to trace the soft skin on her waist. Chelsea put her head on my shoulder and buried her lips in my neck. I thought I might die.

By the time we reached my hotel room, we were both frantic. After shutting the door, I pushed Chelsea up against it and kissed her hard. She met my enthusiasm and shoved her hands beneath my shirt. I pulled my lips away from hers long enough to help her unbutton it. She slid it over my shoulders and dropped it to the floor.

"I think you have an amazing body," Chelsea whispered, running her hands from my shoulders to my chest. She licked her lips, then looked up at me.

I leaned down and started kissing her again. Then I lifted her by her hips, and she wrapped her legs around my waist. I wanted to enjoy Chelsea, but I was so desperate to have her I would have taken her right there, up against the door, if I hadn't managed to calm myself enough to walk over to the bed.

I laid her in front of me while I stood at the end of the bed. She gazed up at me, her eyes so sweet and trusting, her mouth curled into a soft smile, and I felt my chest constrict.

The moment hung in the air. My body froze as my

mind registered something important was happening to me.

But before I could figure it out, Chelsea pulled off her shirt, flinging it to the ground. Then she sat up just enough to unhook her bra, threw that off too, and fell back onto the bed. Her lying there, looking like a goddess on the bed in front me, completely distracted me from whatever had been happening before.

I pulled her jeans and panties off, slowly, watching her face the whole time. Then I fell to the floor at the end of the bed, hooked my hands behind her knees, slid her toward me, and draped her legs over my shoulders. I licked and sucked at her with my tongue while my hands slid slowly up and down the smooth skin at her thighs.

My senses were on overload, consumed with the feel of her, the taste of her, and the sound of her pleasure. The noises Chelsea made were almost too much for me. I felt as though making her feel these things was what my mouth was literally made for. Lost in a trance of her making, I almost didn't notice when she tugged on my hair.

I looked up to see Chelsea, half sitting on the bed, pulling at me desperately. "Please, Henry. Please. I need you."

I didn't waste any time. I practically leapt out of my own jeans, threw on a condom, and fell on the bed, propping myself up above her. I leaned down and kissed her. She moaned and pulled at my waist, her fingers digging into my flesh. I gave her what she wanted, what we both wanted. I lifted her knees up, spreading her legs wide, and sank into her soft body.

Chelsea's lips found my neck, her hands gripped

my ass, and her breasts pressed against my chest. Once again, I was swimming in the sensations of her. Without any control over my own body, spurred on by her urgency, I surged into her over and over, feeling like each time might be the greatest thing I'd ever felt.

Unable to let my enthusiasm end this too soon, I rolled us both over. Chelsea already controlled my every thought and sensation; she might as well control the speed of our lovemaking as well.

She gave me a deep, urgent kiss before sitting up on her knees. Her hands ran over my chest, and her perfect mouth curved in a sinful smile. I loved this playful side of Chelsea. I had to get her naked to fully bring it out, but once it emerged, everything got so much hotter.

"You want me to come, don't you, Henry?" she purred.

I could only nod, hoping to express with my eyes how very much I wanted that.

She moved on top of me. At first, she focused on me, watching my face as she produced involuntary changes—my eyes growing wide and narrowing, clenching closed, my mouth dropping open, then closing, then chomping down on my lower lip.

Eventually though, the sensations running through her own body became too much for her. She threw her head back, moaning as she increased our pace. I gripped her hips and pumped up into her as she began to shiver with her orgasm. And as she came around me, I completely lost it, giving her everything I had.

****

"I don't understand why you have go," I whined as I watched Chelsea button her jeans just moments after

159

we'd finished having what was undeniably the most explosive and meaningful sex of my life.

Her back to me, I could see her chest move as she took a deep breath. After a beat, she turned around. "I should have said this a while ago. I should have…"

I sat up in the bed. "What?"

She took another deep breath and looked away from me. "We have to end this."

"What? Why?" I bolted out of the bed and stood at its foot, naked and anxious.

Chelsea met my gaze. "Remember we said we'd end it, like that." She snapped her fingers. "Well, the time has come."

I didn't know what was going on with me, but I *did* know I didn't want this to end. "Why?"

She took another breath and looked away from me again, her gaze landing on the silent television sitting on top of the dresser. "We have to stick to the rules, Henry."

I took a step back from her as I realized what was happening. "You're interested in someone," I said quietly, realization hitting me like a cement truck.

Chelsea's head snapped up, and for a split second, she looked surprised. Then she nodded. My knees tried to buckle, and I locked them beneath me.

"Who?" I asked weakly.

"Not important."

"Bullshit!" I shouted before I could contain my reaction. "I mean, damn." I ran my hand through my hair. "I thought we were best friends. I thought you could tell me anything."

Chelsea was way calmer than me. She moved toward me, putting a hand on my shoulder. "And I will.

But not right now. We need to take a little time to adjust. After all, our friendship is the most important thing, right?"

I nodded.

"So, let's take care of it. Let's just adjust to this first. Then we'll talk. And I'll tell you everything."

"Okay," I said, feeling like I was being coerced into something I did *not* want to do.

Chelsea kissed my cheek and walked out the door, leaving me naked in the middle of the room, feeling like I'd just lost my best friend.

****

One week, one day ago—Portland, Oregon

"Surprise!" Chelsea shouted as she pulled her hand away from my face.

I looked out the open door of the van and up at the marquee sign above the doors to the venue. The words "Ten Frozen Toes" graced it. "No way!"

"Happy birthday!" Tom said from the driver's seat, just before getting out of the van.

I hopped out onto the sidewalk to join him, Chelsea at my side. Aside from the artificial light, it was dark as hell out there, thanks to the cloudy, starless night. It made the sign stand out even more. "We're going to a Toes concert?"

"You like?" Chelsea asked.

I turned to look at her. Her face was lit up, not by the dim lights of the street but by her own internal glow.

"I love it," I told her. "I've been a fan of the band for years, but I've never seen them in concert."

"I know," Chelsea said smugly.

"Not to wreck your birthday," Tom said, reaching

beside me into the van. "But we do have a permit to film." He pulled a bag out and hefted it onto his shoulders.

I rolled my eyes. "Figures."

Chelsea gave Tom a stern look. "Easy B-roll only, some simple sound takes. Nothing elaborate. We're here to celebrate Henry's birthday, not put him to work."

"Sure thing. Come on." Tom tossed the keys to a valet and walked into the concert hall through the front door.

We appeared to be early for the show. Only a handful of people milled about in the lobby, and a small line was forming at the ticket window. I followed Tom and Chelsea as they walked through the lobby toward closed doors that led to the theater.

I looked around at the art deco lobby of the venue while Tom talked to someone on staff. So I wasn't paying attention to the conversation until I heard the guy Tom was talking to say, "Wait here, just for a moment."

He said it kind of loudly, so I turned my head to see him staring at me. Then the guy disappeared. "What's going on, Tom?" I asked.

"I don't know. We have a permit. But the guy got all weird when he saw *you*."

"Maybe he doesn't like you," Chelsea said to me, a snarky look on her face.

I rolled my eyes at her. I liked that we were back to bantering, so I suppressed my smile. "Lots of people don't like me. They say I'm prickly."

"Hmmm. Good description," she quipped.

A few minutes later, the guy returned. Again, he

addressed me. "Come with me, please, sir."

Sir? What the hell was this? I looked at Tom, but he just shrugged and followed the guy through a side door. I gestured for Chelsea to go in front of me, then I followed her through the door. Even though I'd never been in this particular hall before, I knew from having been in countless concert venues that this route most likely led backstage.

We followed a predictable pattern of hallways and corridors until we were deep inside the backstage area. There were several nondescript doors back there, and the staff member we'd been following stopped in front of one.

"The guys are big fans," he said to me.

"Of the show?" I asked, surprised a rock band watched our lame show on a sub-par cable channel.

"Show?" he asked, looking confused.

Before I could figure out what was going on, the door swung open, and there stood Eddie Trane, lead singer of Ten Frozen Toes. "Holy shit! Henry Rush!" He leaped toward me, his hand extended. Despite my shock, I managed to shake it. "Come on in, man." Eddie pulled the door wide and indicated we should enter.

I put my hand on Chelsea's lower back and ushered her in ahead of me. Tom was at my heels. The small green room looked like a dozen others I'd been in with my dad over the years. A vanity with a mirror and sink sat at one end of the room, a small round table with a couple of chairs in the center, and a worn couch shoved in the far corner with a battered end table beside it.

"Man, it is good to meet you," Eddie said to me. "Hey, John," he called at the staff member. "Bring the other guys in. Tell them he's here."

I suddenly realized that, while I'd come here to see a band I liked perform, I'd just become the center of attention. My stomach curled, and I turned to Tom. He frowned and mouthed, "I'm sorry."

"I have to tell you, Henry, I'm a huge fan of your dad's. *Huge.* We all are. He has seriously influenced our music."

I'd turned my attention back to Eddie with these words. I knew my movements were wooden, as was the smile on my face, no doubt. I tried to loosen my muscles as Eddie insisted I sit on the couch. Chelsea plopped down next to me, and that's where we remained as the rest of the band tumbled into the room.

I had just finished shaking all their hands and accepting their compliments on my dad's music when I felt Chelsea's hand slip into mine. I wrapped her small palm in mine and turned to look at her. She gave me the sweetest smile. And for the first time since we walked into that room, I felt like I could breathe.

We sat there for at least half an hour. I tuned the entire thing out. I desperately wanted to continue enjoying this band and their music. Which meant I needed to sit there, smile, and daydream, blocking out their inane chatter. And that is exactly what I did.

When it was finally over, we were escorted back to the concert hall, now teeming with people. The crowd didn't seem to notice me, thank God, as we made our way to an inconspicuous spot at one end of the hall.

"Was it bad?" Chelsea asked, her face close to my ear as I leaned against the wall.

I shrugged.

"Come on, talk to me," she urged.

I turned to her. She was looking at me like she used

to. I really liked that. So I looped my arm around her waist and pulled her closer to me. She didn't resist. Then I moved my head down, using the noisy concert hall as an excuse to get my mouth close to hers.

"I went on my first tour with my dad at fifteen. It was my idea. I begged him to go. My parents spent weeks debating it, then when they finally decided to let me go, they spent even more time 'preparing me' for it. I thought they were being ridiculously overcautious. But it turns out, they weren't."

"So you were exposed to a lot of sex, drugs, and rock 'n' roll?" she asked.

"A little. But that wasn't a big deal. There wasn't any more of that than at my high school. No. The problem was the way people treated me. I'd been pretty sheltered as a kid. I went to school in Malibu. Hell, half the kids I knew had famous parents. And I was nerdy, so…aside from the girl problems I already told you about…I wasn't a big deal. But on tour, everywhere we went, I was nearly as famous as my dad. It's like with those guys." I point my finger in the direction of the backstage area. "They treat me like *I'm* the rock star. But, in fact, they are all star struck over my genes."

Chelsea laughed. "Your genes?"

"Yeah. They want to be in my presence because in their minds I am the progeny of a rock god."

"Your dad *is* a rock god," she pointed out, her lip curled up at one end.

I leaned closer to her. "Yeah. But he's just my dad."

She smiled at me, and I was completely mesmerized by it. So I leaned down and kissed her. But she pulled away quickly and stuck her finger over my lips. "You're breaking the rules, Henry," she said, tutting at me.

I let out a deep sigh and turned my gaze to the stage just as Ten Frozen Toes appeared beneath the spotlight.

****

Three days ago—San Francisco, California

It had been a full week since Chelsea had told me she had a thing for someone else, and I still didn't know who it was. It had been seven long nights since I'd last had Chelsea warm and soft beneath me in bed, and I still didn't understand why.

I'd tried to be patient. I didn't want to harm our friendship. So I hadn't pushed the issue. But in truth, we weren't the same anyway. The friendship we so desperately tried to keep intact was just a shell of what it had once been. And I wanted to know why.

So the night before we were supposed to leave for LA, I confronted her, demanding answers. We only had a handful of days left to shoot the show. It would all be over after we shot the final scenes at my dad's concert. Then, Chelsea and I would both come back to San Francisco. I'd move out of my uncle's place and get an apartment with the money from the show. I'd bury myself in there trying to write some articles or stories I could sell. And Chelsea would go back to her life and her career.

And I hoped we would see each other. I hoped we would hang out, and talk, and yeah, maybe even have sex occasionally. I hoped things would be how they'd been for the last several months.

But if that was going to happen, I needed to fix this. And I couldn't fix it if I didn't know what was wrong.

"We have to talk," I said, shutting the door of my room behind me.

We'd been out in the living room watching a baseball game with my uncle just before I'd pulled her in here. The game wrapped up, and she was getting ready to go home. Tomorrow, we'd be on a plane to LA, and we wouldn't have a chance to talk, maybe not again until after we came back to San Francisco. I couldn't wait that long.

"Okay." She sat down on the edge of the bed and stared down at her hands in her lap, looking very much like she was about to be tortured.

I sat down next to her. "Things are weird between us, Chels. We need to fix it," I told her, having already decided to be just completely straightforward.

She sighed. "How do you think we can fix it, Henry?" She still wasn't looking at me, and there was something fatalistic in her voice.

"Well, for starters, I think you should tell me who you've got a thing for." Silence—deep silence—greeted my suggestion. "Chels?"

Finally, she looked up at me. "Henry...I...there isn't someone else."

"You lied to me?" I couldn't believe it.

"No." She shook her head. "No. I didn't lie."

"You're not making any sense. You said we had to cut things off between us because you were into someone," I reminded her.

Suddenly, she grabbed me by the shoulders and shook me. "Why are you so damn stupid, Henry!"

"What the hell?"

"I have a thing for *you*, Henry! You! You

dumbass!"

I sat there, staring at her. She let go of me and stood. I followed her with my eyes as she paced in front of me. "I don't—what?" I asked, feeling utterly flummoxed.

"Ugh," she said, throwing her hands in the air. She came to a stop in front me. "I have feelings for you, Henry. And I can't do this 'friends with benefits' bullshit with you anymore. I want *more*. I want the whole thing, Henry. I want a relationship." She stuck her hands on her hips. "There. I said it. Now what?"

I stared at her. I had absolutely no idea how to respond to this. So I said nothing.

"You don't have anything to say?" she asked, clearly frustrated.

"Chels, I…I don't know what to say."

"Why don't you tell me how you feel, Henry?"

"I…I liked things the way they were," I told her honestly.

I could see immediately I'd made a mistake. Her lips pressed together, her eyes narrowed, and she leaned forward menacingly. "I just bet you did," she said in a low voice. "You got what you wanted without any 'complications.' "

"Um…yeah. I thought that's what we both wanted," I said defensively.

"Maybe once, but not anymore. I want *more*, Henry," she said. "How could you not want that, too? After everything. After…" She straightened and ran her hand over her face. "I'm an idiot. Why would I ever think I could get to you?" she said, more to herself than to me. "Why would I ever—God, between my own building self-esteem and your mom…Jesus, I actually believed…"

She pivoted on her heel and headed for the door.

I stood. "Where are you going?"

She turned to look at me, one hand on the door handle. "Goodbye, Henry."

And she walked out, just like that.

****

Present day—Los Angeles, California

"Honestly, Dad, I'm not sure what even went wrong."

"I think it's obvious, Buddy. She fell in love with you."

I hang my head in my hands for a moment, letting that really sink in. I know he is right, maybe I'd even known it for a while. But over the last two days as I'd traveled through LA with Billy-the-replacement shooting the final scenes for the show, I'd chosen to ignore that and focus on my anger over what I'd lost.

Chelsea certainly made it clear she had feelings during our confrontation at my uncle's house. And when she didn't show up at the airport the next morning, I'd known she wasn't going to be joining us in LA. She didn't answer my texts. She didn't answer anyone's texts. She didn't pick up her phone. Nothing.

I'd gone through the motions for the last two days. I'd also been avoiding my family. I'd stayed in a hotel and promised I'd visit once all the shooting was over. Then, on my way over to the concert to meet up with my dad, I'd had to face reality. I had asked myself what would make Chelsea disappear from her life like that? What would make her abandon her career, leave me high and dry, and hide out like a criminal?

She had fallen for me.

"The question is," my dad says, recalling my attention. I pull my head out of my hands and look up at him. "How do you feel about her?"

"I want her." The words tumble out of my mouth without thought.

"But what are you willing to *give* her?"

The question, asked in my father's gentle baritone, sounds far more innocuous than it is. But I've known for a while now I would have to face it.

I stand. "I can give her what she wants."

My father looks up at me, and unexpectedly, he looks skeptical. "Are you sure?"

"Of course, I'm sure, Dad. I'm going to San Francisco. I'm going to get her back."

My dad stands up and puts his hand on my shoulder. "I'm not going to talk you out of it. But…"

"What?" I ask, feeling impatient with his sudden resistance to what I'm sure he had been trying to push me toward this whole time.

He hesitates, his eyebrows scrunched up. Then he pulls me into a hug. "Nothing, Buddy." He pats my back and pulls back. "Travel safe."

Chapter 17

Present day—Los Angeles, California
Chelsea

I am officially an idiot. This is the thought going through my head as I stand in front of the imposing security guard. His arms are folded over his chest, and he looks as though protecting the large metal door at his back is what he was born to do.

I've had plenty of time over the past three hours to figure out how I would get past this particular roadblock. After Candace and Jack had convinced me I should go after Henry, I'd jumped right into the task.

Having realized I'd never actually given Henry the chance to absorb how I had changed the rules on him, I wanted to go back and alter the conversation. I wanted to give Henry a chance to answer my demands. I wanted to see if I could still have him.

After two days of utter misery, I'd gone to Jack and Candace looking for hope. And they'd given it to me. Jack had asked one question: Why had I assumed Henry's hesitation to immediately declare everything should change between us meant he didn't want me? I hadn't been able to answer that question. And it had made me realize I hadn't given him a chance.

It was Candace who suggested I go after Henry. After all, Jack had run from her once, and that's what she'd done, she'd tracked him down. And, for her, it had all worked out. She got a husband, a dog, and as I'd learned today, she was going to have a kid in about seven months.

Candace was able to order the corporate jet without me having to call my dad and explain my situation. That was a nightmare I didn't need. So I'd packed a small bag, boarded the plane, flown to LA, then taken a cab to the venue where Henry's dad and uncle were playing a concert tonight.

And while I'd flown, I'd contemplated exactly what I was going to say to Henry when I saw him. What I didn't do was figure out how to get into the stupid building.

I'd tried to call Tom from the cab, but he wasn't answering his phone. And now that I'm standing outside the building, I know why. It's louder than hell in there. The music, which I'm pretty sure is Hank Tolk and his band, is spilling out of the arena and into the night air.

My pass had undoubtedly been given to Billy, who Tom informed me yesterday had taken over my duties when I was a no show. So I have no way in.

"I'm Henry Rushton's best friend," I try.

The guard harrumphs at me.

"No seriously. I've been trying to call and text him." I hold up my phone to show my unanswered texts. "But I'm thinking maybe he doesn't get reception in there."

The guard leans forward and looks at my screen. It's warmer here than in San Francisco, and he's wearing just a T-shirt that shows off his thick biceps. Add that to his scruffy face and deep voice, and I'm a little intimidated. Especially when he says, "How do I even know that's his number? It just says Henry. That could be anyone. Or, hell, you could be a stalker."

I scroll down on my phone to show him the dozen or so unanswered texts Henry sent me over the last two days. "No, see, these are from him. He wants to talk to me. He wants to see me." The guard leans back and twists his mouth up in a grimace. I sigh. "So there's no way in?"

He rolls his eyes. "Give me a minute. I'll ask around," he says. Then he holds one hand up to me. "But *you* stay right here."

I nod, and he opens the large steel door. But as he disappears inside, the door doesn't fully latch behind him. It only takes me a split second to make my decision. Then, I wrench the door open and bolt inside.

The guard is leaning on the doorjamb of a small room immediately inside, talking to another guard. I run past him and keep running, even as I hear shouting and the sounds of pursuit coming from behind me.

I am in a labyrinth of nondescript hallways, white-painted brick flying by me as I desperately search for something that will help—a sign, a person, anything. And then I hit it. Literally.

I run directly into the largest human being I've ever seen. My comparatively tiny body bounces off a massive chest. I would have fallen straight back onto the floor except for a pair of enormous hands reaching out and catching me, one grasping each shoulder.

I look up, way up, to see an older, larger version of Henry staring down at me. He smiles and says, "You must be Chelsea."

The security guard rushes up to us then. "I'm sorry,

Mr. Rush. She came out of—"

"Don't worry about it, Charlie. This is Henry's girlfriend. Didn't she tell you?"

Poor Charlie is nearly as much at a loss as I am. Henry's dad lets the guy off the hook. "I'm going to take Chelsea to my green room, Charlie. Thanks." Then he wraps one arm around my shoulders and turns us both so we are walking the opposite direction down the hallway. "I was just going out to watch Hank's set when I saw you. Good karma, huh?"

I nod. "Um, thank you, Mr...um." I hesitate. Do I call him Mr. Rush, which is his stage name, or Mr. Rushton, which I know is his real name, because it demonstrates how close I am to his son?

Before I can figure it out, he helps me, again. "Call me Sean. I have to say, I am pleasantly surprised to see you here, Chelsea. Henry said you'd basically disappeared on him." He stops in front of a brown door and opens it. He ushers me inside and closes the door behind him.

The music is further muted in here. There is a couch, a small table, and a vanity with a big mirror and a sink. But no Henry.

"Please, have a seat," he says, extending his arm to the couch.

I sit down stiffly while Sean freaking Rush folds his massive frame into a tiny metal chair across from me.

"I don't suppose I'm going to get you to talk to me, huh?" he says lightly.

"I'm sorry. I'm just a little...um...How did you know it was me?" I ask.

"My wife has about a dozen selfies of you and her

getting plastered at the bar in Denver. She showed them to me."

"Oh…um…that makes sense."

He leans back in his chair and looks at me. He is big, handsome, and slightly terrifying. In person he's larger, yes, but also somehow softer. I think that's because he looks so much like Henry. And I love Henry. I imagine watching him grow older, looking more and more like his father each year. And my heart cracks.

"Is Henry here?" I ask.

"Hmmm. About that. He *was* here. We talked, and then he left."

"He left?" I can feel myself panicking.

"Yes. He went after you."

"*What?*"

"Apparently, you both had the same idea at the same time because he left here to go to San Francisco and find you."

My heart hammers in my chest. "What…? When was this?"

"A little before I went on stage. Then I performed and just got off about twenty minutes ago. Hank's on now. So, um, maybe two hours ago. He was going to catch a plane…" He pulls a small smartphone out of his pocket and looks at it. "He should be landing in SF soon."

"Shit," I say, feeling defeated.

Sean chuckles. "I'll just tell him to come right back." He types a text message on his phone, and for a moment, I am completely distracted by trying to figure out how he pushes the right buttons on such a tiny phone with his huge fingers.

When he's done, he shoves the phone back in his pocket and smiles at me. "He'll come back, and you two will work this out. In the meantime, you can hang out with me."

Great. I can hang out with a world-renowned rock star and act like it's no big deal for the next few hours, while I wait for his son to arrive and hopefully not reject me and break my heart.

"Um, okay…I should probably check on the Trek crew, too."

"They're gone." He waves his hand. "They got a few shots of me on stage and took off. Since Henry is gone, they gave up. Besides Tom said he had what he needs for the show."

I am at a loss for words. So I just stare at Sean Rush.

"You wanna watch Hank's show?" he asks me.

I nod, like the pathetic, drooling, star-struck moron I am.

****

In one of the most surreal scenes of my life to date, I am sitting in Sean Rush's living room. Dani has just served me a tall glass of green liquid she calls the "Baby Special." It has more alcohol in it than I should ever drink in one sitting.

"Try it," she encourages, sitting down on the coffee table and stretching out her legs so they rest on the couch beside her husband. I am sitting at the other end of the couch and watch as he immediately takes her bare feet in his hands and begins to gently rub them.

I take a sip of the drink and find it refreshingly sweet and smooth. "This is dangerous," I tell her.

"If you two get wasted and leave me here to

176

explain it to Henry…" Sean says.

Dani smiles at him. "You'll what?"

He shakes his head.

"Chelsea," Dani says. "I'm so glad you came."

"You miss me?" I ask her, harkening back to our easy camaraderie in Denver.

"Definitely! You need to stay for a few days and hang out with me and Bell. We'll have a blast!"

"I get the impression Henry hates that you two are BFFs," Sean says.

Dani waves her hand at him. "Whatever, Henry will just have to deal."

"Agreed," I say, clinking my glass to hers.

Sean chuckles.

"Okay, so. Let's talk about why you're here," Dani says.

"I already made her spill her guts, Baby," Sean tells her.

Dani was not at the concert. Apparently, she'd been helping Henry's sister, Gloria, with something instead. So I'd spent Hank's entire set sitting next to Sean backstage. Afterward, I'd ridden back to Malibu with him. Ten minutes after we'd arrived at the house, Dani finally made an appearance. And now here I am, sitting with the two of them on the couch.

I have to pinch myself to make sure I am awake.

"Yeah, but *I* didn't get to hear it," she complains. "At least give me the short version."

I lean back into the corner of the very comfortable couch and take another sip of my drink. "Well, I managed to completely screw up the confrontation with Henry." Which makes me feel like an ass, because she and I had discussed it in detail in Denver, and then I'd had three weeks to practice it. And I'd still completely fucked it up.

"How?" she asks.

"Well, I didn't actually give him a chance to…um…respond."

"Huh" is her only answer.

"I imagine it was not unlike conversations we've had, Baby," Sean says to his wife.

She nods, a serious look on her face.

"So…um…when he gets here…" I begin, fumbling to figure out how to ask their advice.

But I never get the chance because the sound of the lock being turned in the front door, by someone who obviously has a key, jolts me. From where we are sitting on the couch, all three of us have a clear view of the entryway. And as I watch Henry walk in, I stiffen.

He stops in the doorway and looks at me for a long beat before tossing his backpack in the foyer and walking fully into the living room.

"Hey, Mom. Hey, Dad," he says casually. Then his voice changes, becoming lower. "Hi, Chels."

"Well, now that you've finally managed to catch up with each other," Sean says, standing, "we'll leave you two alone." He pulls Dani up, too.

Dani smiles and walks over to Henry. She kisses him on the cheek, grabs her drink off the coffee table, winks at me, and walks out of the room, Sean right behind her.

"We need to talk," Henry says.

Chapter 18

"Yeah." My eyes dart to the sliding glass door at the other end of the room. "Can we go out in the backyard?"

Henry grins. "You want to see my childhood backyard, don't you?"

I nod.

Henry holds his hand out to me. It is invitation for closeness. And I take it. Then we walk together out into the warm Malibu night. "How was the concert?" he asks me.

I sit down on a porch swing overlooking the pool. "It was fun. Kind of…surreal, but fun."

Henry sits down beside me and drapes an arm over my shoulders. I cuddle in closer, desperate to feel his warmth surrounding me again. "My dad likes you."

"You could tell that in ten seconds?"

"Well, yeah. But he also told me."

I look up at him. "I've been with him nonstop since I got here. When, exactly, did this conversation occur?"

He chuckles. "By text. The point is, you've won my parents over, Chels."

"Is that good or bad?"

He seems to ponder this for a moment. Then he says, "I guess it's good. I can't think of any reason it would be bad."

"So, um, I guess we should talk about our shit," I

tell him.

"I'm sorry I wasn't responsive the other day, Chels. You just kind of took me by surprise."

"I know. I realized later I didn't really give you a chance to...deal. I had worked myself up by then, you know."

"I guess I don't know. Why were you so worked up? You were upset before we even talked."

"I was," I admit. "I had convinced myself I could never have what I wanted with you."

Henry shifts in his seat so he can see me better. "Why? Why would you think that before even asking me?"

I shrug, and suddenly feeling shy, I look away from Henry, focusing my gaze on the pool. It is bathed in a soft green glow created by the lights buried within the still waters. Henry waits while I work up the nerve to tell him the truth.

"Okay, here it is," I say. "When it comes to being friends, you and I are a perfect match. But when it comes to romance...we're not."

"Why?"

"I'm not in your league."

Henry grasps my chin between his thumb and forefinger and forces me to turn my head and look at him. "That. Is. Ridiculous." His voice is quiet and firm.

"Not from my perspective."

Henry frowns at me.

"But I am pretty much in the process of deciding I am as great as I want to be. And that, whatever hang-ups I have, I shouldn't underestimate myself."

"Goddamn right," he growls, lowering his mouth to mine and taking me into a deep kiss. He pulls away and looks me in the eye. "Chelsea, you are a beautiful, sexy, smart, witty, amazing woman." He takes a deep breath. "And I want to have a real relationship with you. I want to give you *more*."

I attack him. Our mouths clash together. Our hands start to roam. We are both breathing hard, and the porch swing is starting to move. "We need to go somewhere, Henry," I pant.

He pulls away and swiftly gets to his feet, taking me along with him. "My room," he says simply.

He is already dragging me toward the house when I start to protest. "Your childhood room, really?"

He doesn't pause in his march. We slide through the door and across the living room. "Yep."

"But, I mean, your parents…"

"My room is on the opposite side of the house." He makes a right and heads down a hallway. "And it's a big house, Chels."

I quit arguing and follow more willingly. Near the end of the hall, we hook into a large room. It doesn't look like much like a childhood room. In fact, it is a lot like the room my parents still keep for me at their house. There are traces of a growing boy having once occupied it. An accent wall is painted navy blue. A corkboard still sits in one corner over a small wooden desk. But the corkboard is empty now, and the desk holds laptop cords and battery chargers. The bed is large, California king probably, and is flanked by two sophisticated bedside tables. A matching dresser sits near the closet.

Henry pulls his shirt off as soon as we enter the room and throws it on the floor. Then he reaches for me. I sidestep him. "You sure you want to do this in your parents' house?" I tease. I take my glasses off and place them on the dresser. Then I pull my own shirt off and throw it on top of his on the floor.

He reaches for me again, but I manage to snake away, backing toward the bed. Then I pull my bra off. Much to my delight, Henry's eyes grow wide and desire plays on his face. He manages to get hold of me. He kisses me hard and pushes me back on the bed.

I laugh as Henry pulls my hands over my head and buries his face in my neck. "It kind of feels like we're naughty teenagers," I tell him, practically giggling.

Henry chuckles and looks up at me. "I am a *way* better lover now, Chels."

"Lucky me."

****

I am sprawled out on the bed, my head resting on Henry's chest, when I open my eyes. Henry runs his hands through my hair, and I pull myself up so I can see him. "Morning," I whisper.

"Good morning."

"We're totally naked in your parents' house," I say.

"You are overly obsessed with that," he tells me, smiling. "We're in our late twenties, Chels."

"*You* are in your late twenties, I am still in my *mid* twenties," I point out, just to be a pain in the ass.. "It's just, all of the sexual experimenting I did in my teenage years, behind my parents' back in my childhood bedroom, kinda affects my thinking, even now."

"Well, we're adults. And besides, this isn't a convent. My dad is a rock star, you know."

I run my fingers through his long, silky, black hair. "You think you'll be as hot as your dad when you get older?"

Henry groans. "Please. Do *not* talk to me about how hot my dad is when I'm in bed naked with you."

Suddenly, I get serious. "Shit. I'm sorry, Henry. I forgot about your hang-up."

"Hang-up? Oh, yeah. I did, too."

"You did?"

"Yeah. I wasn't worrying about that just now, though. I was just jealous." He runs one hand lightly over my breast.

"Jealous?"

"Hmmm. I'd rather you *only* find *me* hot, at least when you're in bed with me." He leans in to pull my earlobe between his teeth.

Then, much to my dismay, a knock sounds on the door. Both Henry and I stiffen.

"Yes?" Henry calls.

"Henry, we're having breakfast. You and Chelsea should join us," Dani says from behind the door.

"Okay, Mom. We'll be there in a few."

We are both completely still, listening hard as the sound of her footsteps fades away. Then I bury my head in Henry's chest and giggle in a way I haven't done in years.

"Come on," Henry says, pulling out from beneath me and standing beside the bed. "We better go have awkward family time."

We both get dressed and walk out into the hall hand in hand. Henry leads me through a spacious dining room, but to my surprise it is empty. I pause there, but Henry tugs on my hand and leads me into the kitchen.

A six-person oval table sits near a bay window in one corner of the spacious kitchen, and that's where Dani sits, sipping on coffee. Sean is at the stove, his back to us.

"Good morning. Have a seat, Chelsea," Dani says, gesturing to the chair beside her.

Instead of sitting down with us, Henry goes to the counter to pour two cups of coffee. After bringing me one, he wanders back over the refrigerator and grabs the cream for me. I like that Henry knows how I take my coffee. And I like that I don't have to ask for him to accommodate me. I smile to myself. Dani catches me.

"What are you making, Dad?" Henry asks.

Sean turns around. "Guess."

"Pancakes and bacon."

Sean smiles and salutes his son with a spatula before turning back. I pour the cream into my mug and try not think about how freaking surreal this all is.

Dani examines us over the lip of her mug. "Sleep all right?"

"Yeah," Henry mumbles. "Jetlagged after all that going back and forth last night," he says, winking at me.

"Gloria wants to know if you two are staying in Malibu for a while. She wants to see you."

Henry looks at me. "I'm not in a hurry to get back to SF. Are you, Chels?"

I shrug. "I don't have a job anymore, so I guess not."

Henry frowns. "I bet you could get your job at Trek back. In fact, I could call Steve and explain that it was all my fault—"

I hold my hand up to stop him. "It's okay. Tom is retiring after this gig, and you're all done. I would be miserable. I'll find something else."

Henry looks at me long and hard. "Are you sure?"

I nod. "Let's stay here for a few days." I like the idea of seeing Malibu through Henry's eyes. I want to make him take me to his old haunts. And, most of all, I want to meet his big, complicated family.

Sean walks over to the table, a giant stack of pancakes piled onto a plate that is balanced in one hand and a jumble of crispy bacon nestled in a dish in the other. He sets them down on the table and takes the other seat next to Dani. Sean doesn't speak, he just starts filling the plates. Dani and Henry seem to know what the cues are, and they start passing the food around, too.

"This is my contribution," Dani says, pulling a dish toward her from the center of the table and uncovering it. "Fruit salad." She eyes her husband. "*Someone* has make sure there's a bit of nutrition in our meals."

"Bacon is good for you," Sean mumbles before digging into his breakfast.

We eat in companionable silence for a while. The only sounds are utensils hitting ceramic and nearly burnt bacon crunching. It is a good meal, and I am feeling happy and relaxed. Then Dani ruins it.

"So, where do you go from here?" she asks, pointing between Henry and me with her fork.

"Really, Mom?" Henry asks. After giving her an incredulous glance, he turns his gaze toward his father. And I can see by the look in his eyes he is seeking help.

Sean puts his fork down and leans back in his chair. And for a split second, I think he *is* going to help. But instead, he says, "Good question."

Henry lets out a deep, exasperated sigh and turns to me. "Sorry. I didn't know how weird they'd be. I rarely bring girls home."

"Try never," Dani says.

"Didn't I bring Rochelle home once?"

"I guess. But that was a long-ass time ago, and you're trying to deflect," Dani says.

Henry abandons his breakfast and folds his arms over his chest, looking like a virtual clone of the man sitting across from him. "Well, we're going to stay here for a few days and hang out unless you drive us away with your crazy questions."

Dani rolls her eyes, but she doesn't push the issue any further. Instead, she says, "Chelsea, let's have a girls' night out tomorrow."

Henry and Sean both groan.

Chapter 19

Four months later—San Francisco
Henry

"I love you, Henry," she says, stroking my cheek and looking into my eyes.

We've just finished making love, and she's warm and soft against me. I pull her closer, squeezing hard, hoping I can convey how I feel *this way* because for some bizarre reason, I just can't seem to say the words back to her.

Chelsea, her head now buried in my neck, sighs heavily, but she doesn't complain. This is the third time she's been overcome with emotion, all after we've had sex, and told me she loves me. And each time I've responded the same way, with silence.

We don't talk about it afterward. We never do. We just cuddle and kiss and fall asleep. But this time it's morning, and I'm worried. I have to go soon. If I get right up, without smoothing things over in some way, I could leave her hurting.

I pull back and look at her, tracing her lips with my fingers. She is amazing. So I tell her that. "You are so beautiful, Chels. Sometimes I feel like I'm living in a dream, waking up to you every morning."

"About that," she says, propping herself up on her elbow. "I either need a roommate, or I need you to just officially move in and start helping me with rent."

She's turned all business on me quickly, and I don't like it.

"I will help pay the rent," I tell her.

I can afford it now that my articles, written about the various places we visited while shooting the show, are selling. My money from the show is also still sitting in the bank. And I don't pay my uncle anything to hang onto my stuff and keep a room empty for me while I spend every night at Chelsea's.

But this isn't about money, not really. In fact, Chelsea doesn't even need to pay rent because she lives in a building owned by her family's company. She just insists on paying rent on principle.

This conversation is the result of two important and stressful issues for Chelsea. And I know all about it. First, she's worried the movie she's currently working on won't get aired. I know it will, but my reassurances won't help. She'll relax once it actually all works out.

But she is also stressed out because she isn't sure where we really stand. If I officially move in with her, it will mean something to her. And Chelsea needs to know where we are.

The problem is, *I* don't know where we are. I am happy every single day with Chelsea. And I don't want to mess with that. Labels and decisions—these are things that could really screw it all up. So, I've been avoiding them. Chelsea has been putting up with it. And I love her for that.

Hell, I just plain love her. I know it. I've known it since the morning we sat at my parents' kitchen table and ate breakfast. I look at Chelsea the way my dad looks at my mom. I'd realized it right then.

And the next night, when my mom, sister, and aunt took Chelsea out, my dad told me he'd seen it, too. I'd simply nodded. I was well aware of what had happened to me. I just didn't want to say it out loud.

Chelsea looks at the clock beside the bed. "Damn. You have to get going. Don't you have a meeting with an editor this morning?"

"Yeah," I say, reluctantly letting her go so I can pull myself out of bed. "What about you? You think you'll finish polishing up that short you made for PBS?"

"I think I'll get it done today. But," she shrugs, "I have until the end of the week. And I have a lunch date today."

After this declaration, she hops out of bed and goes to the dresser. She pulls underwear and a bra out of the top drawer and head for the bathroom. I follow her. "Lunch date? With Jack?"

She puts her underwear on the back of the toilet and turns on the water in the shower. "No."

"Candace?"

"No."

"Your parents?"

She shakes her head.

I am getting frustrated. "Hayden?"

"Nope," she practically chirps. Then she hits the button to make the water come pouring out of the shitty showerhead she's been putting up with for years now and steps in.

I follow her. "Then who?"

"You haven't met him." She reaches for the shampoo, hands it to me, and proceeds to get her hair wet.

"And...who is *he*?"

"Gary," she says, swiveling to turn her back to me.

I am in the middle of lathering the shampoo up in my hands when my whole body goes still. "Wait...Gary, your ex-boyfriend?"

"Mm-hmmm. Well, kind of. We were never actually dating, you know. We were just friends with benefits."

I feel like I just got punched in the gut.

Since I've gone still and am not running the shampoo through her hair, as she expects, she turns around to look at me. "What?"

"Why are you seeing Gary?"

"What do you mean, why? I told you we were still friends. We made a lunch date. It's not a big deal, Henry."

I will myself to move, turning her around and massaging the shampoo through her hair. "Yeah. Cool. Have fun."

****

I am officially a major ass. I've actually followed my girlfriend to her lunch date. After our shower, while she was getting dressed, I'd peeked in her day planner and found out when and where she was meeting Gary. Then, after my morning meeting, I went to the small café to stalk them.

I stand in an alcove across the street from the restaurant. I'm leaning casually against the building at my back as if it's perfectly normal to stand here and stare at all the patrons as they come and go.

I know this is awful. I know it's dishonest, not to mention horrible and ridiculous. But here I am, anyway. I can't seem to help myself. I am so insanely jealous right now.

Gary is the one person I fear the most. I know he and Chelsea are still close friends. And I know he recently broke up with his girlfriend. She'd spent a few hours on the phone with him a couple of weeks ago after it all went down.

On top of whatever closeness they already share, whatever attraction she holds for him, and whatever kind of sexual tension may still exist between them, I am not giving Chelsea what she needs.

I see Chelsea arrive at the restaurant. She waits outside the door for a few minutes. Then a man approaches her. He is tall and thin with short hair. I can't tell from here if he's handsome, but I suppose it doesn't matter. What matters is what Chelsea thinks of him. I tense when he scoops her up in a hug. She laughs and kisses his cheek, and it grates on my nerves.

They enter the restaurant together. I am torn between trying to find a way to see inside and to do the right thing and leave altogether. I'm just about to bug out, when they reappear. They are accompanied by a waitress who seats them at a small table in the outside area, surrounded by a short metal fence. The table they've been assigned gives me a perfect view of them, and so I stay put, rooted to the ground, this concrete building glued to my back.

I can't hear them, of course, and I know this is pointless. I don't actually believe Chelsea is going to suddenly launch herself out of her seat, kiss Gary passionately, then walk to the nearest hotel with him.

But what I *am* worried about is she'll look at him the way she looks at me most of the time. It's this amazing expression she gets as she gazes down at me after sex, or while we're sitting across the table from one another, or while we're cuddling on the couch. But lately, she's been looking more frustrated than enamored. And it scares the hell out of me.

They are talking and eating, and I'm standing there watching them, like it's a movie, when she scans the area around her. It happens so fast I don't have time to move. And when her eyes lock onto mine, I know I'm screwed.

Chelsea gets up out of her chair in one fluid movement. She turns away from me for a split second to say something to Gary. He looks over at me and frowns. But he stays in his seat as Chelsea walks into the restaurant.

I don't know why I am not fleeing. But I'm not. I hold my ground as Chelsea reappears out of the front door of the restaurant and stands at the edge of the sidewalk directly across from me.

I push off the building at my back and take a step forward as Chelsea looks both ways quickly before jaywalking across the street. She reaches me in a heartbeat, and I stand there, ready to take the punishment I deserve.

She walks right up to me, her face just inches from mine. She looks up and says sternly, "Henry. I don't even have the words."

"I'm sorry," I say simply, unable to come up with any valid excuse for my horrendous behavior.

She turns on her heel and marches right back to Gary.

****

I'm sitting in Chelsea's living room, my leg obsessively bouncing up and down. I'm watching the front door, anticipating Chelsea's return, and I'm scared shitless. I've been waiting about an hour when the door swings open. Chelsea walks inside, slams the door behind her, throws her purse on the floor and stomps over to me, a deep grimace on her face.

"I know you're pissed," I say, "and you have every right to be."

"Well, thank you so much for the permission," she snaps.

"It was a horrible thing to do," I admit.

"Agreed!"

"You are probably considering kicking me to the curb right now. And I wouldn't blame you."

"The thought definitely crossed my mind."

She is standing in front of me, and I'm sitting on the couch. As much as I want to pull her down into my lap, for now, it is probably best she have the upper hand. "So what can I do to convince you to keep me around?"

"Well, you can start with an explanation," she demands, her hands planted on her hips.

"I am crazy, mad in love with you," I say simply. As I say it, I feel like a giant weight has been lifted off my shoulders. And I can't for the life of me figure out why I'd been carrying it around all this time.

Chelsea's mouth drops open, her arms fall to her sides, and she stares at me for a long moment. "What?" she finally says in a whisper.

"I'm in love with you, Chels. I have been for a while. I've just been too stubborn to admit it. I want you. I want you so bad it causes me physical pain sometimes. And because I've never told you, because I've stubbornly refused to take our relationship to the next level, I was risking losing you. So, I was insecure, and I didn't even know it." I take a deep breath. I am talking very fast, and I try to slow myself down. "I was so insecure, Chels, when I got jealous of Gary, I got downright crazy."

She's watching me intently through this speech. And now, as I wind down, a tear slips from her eye. I hold my arms out and she falls into my lap. I pull Chelsea close to me, holding on to her as if my life depends on it. And in a way, it does.

****

Eight months later—Los Angeles, California

This is embarrassing as hell. I guess having spent last year's birthday away from my crazy-ass family, I'd managed to forget how absolutely nutty they get about the occasion.

I officially moved in with Chelsea the very next day after the stalking incident. With each other's encouragement, support, and love, we've both been advancing our careers. I am selling my stories as a freelance writer, and I've recently started writing a novel. Chelsea's short was aired on PBS, and now she's working on a full-length doc for them.

I can't believe how incredibly lucky I am to have spent the last year with Chelsea at my side. And today I am also one year older.

My family is all here, gathered at my parents' place and celebrating as if I'd won the Nobel prize in literature, instead of merely being born on this day. We've already had an elaborate dinner followed by a succulent dessert. Then the ladies had gotten into the cocktails.

Now we've finally retired to one of my favorite

places, the backyard. We're sitting around a bonfire, the orange glow illuminating the dark night. Chelsea is sitting beside me, looking like an angel in a white dress and strappy sandals. The light from the fire bounces off her glasses and reflects her warm smile.

Everyone else has taken up a seat around the fire as well. We're all squeezed in, sitting in a variety of chairs—all except my dad. An empty seat beside me awaits him. And when he does appear, he's carrying three guitar cases. He hands one to my Uncle Hank, he hands me one case, and then lowers himself into the waiting seat with his own battered guitar case.

Chelsea watches with excitement as we pull out the instruments. She's seen us play before, but she never seems to get tired of it. And I'm glad she's excited because tonight is going to be different, and I want her to be paying close attention.

My dad and my uncle are on board with my plan. So they don't mess around. As soon as we're situated, they both start strumming their guitars. I join in and watch the confused look on Chelsea's face.

I think she recognizes the tune in that way people sometimes do. You know you know the song, but your brain doesn't quite kick in until the singing begins.

We drag the intro out a bit, then I start to sing. Chelsea's face begins to glow with a massive smile as I weave out the lyrics to "You're My Best Friend" by Queen.

By the time I finish, she looks like the happiest woman in the world. She's grinning from ear to ear. I hand my guitar blindly to my dad, my gaze still on Chelsea while she claps wildly along with the rest of family. Then I fall to my knees in front her, grasping both of her hands in mine.

Chelsea stills. The background noise from my family quickly becomes a deep silence.

I can hear my own heart beating in my chest. "Chels. You *are* my best friend. And you are also so much more than that. You know I love you. You know I want to be with you all the time. You literally light up my life." I take a deep breath. "I know I didn't jump into our relationship the way you would have liked. And I know it doesn't make for a very good story for our kids. But I'm hoping maybe you could start the story here, with me telling you that you are all I want. You are my present and my future, Chels." The speed of my heart kicks up a notch. "And I'm hoping you will do me the great honor of being my wife."

Chelsea is completely still. She looks like a statue. And I start to worry. I'm pretty sure my entire family is holding their breath. There isn't a single sound out here aside from the crackle of the fire burning up the wood, consuming the bark and cambium.

Time seems to stop until finally Chelsea moves. She throws her arms around me and buries her face in my neck. I feel moisture on my skin and hear a small sob.

"Chels?" I ask, holding her close.

She lifts her head and sniffs. "Yes, Henry. I'll marry you," she says, her voice breaking.

It's as if a wall has collapsed, or a balloon is popped, or time has simply restarted. My family begins to clap and shout and cry out. And I pull Chelsea to me and kiss her, feeling like this crazy ride I got on nearly two years ago has led me to the greatest destination I can imagine.

Epilogue

One year later—Sausalito, California

My wife is incredible.

My wife. She's been that for a little over an hour now. I look over at her and wonder how the hell I got so lucky.

Chelsea throws her head back and laughs at something Tom has just whispered in her ear. I reach out and grasp her hand. She turns her head and smiles at me. It's radiant.

"Did you like the dinner?" she asks me.

I shrug. In truth, I hardly ate any of it. I am still living in that moment when Chelsea and I looked each other in the eye and said, "I do." I'm having a hard time concentrating on the noise and gaiety of the reception. I just want to take Chelsea back to our hotel room and get her naked.

She leans over and kisses me lightly. "I have to go to the little girls' room before we start dancing," she says. Her lips brush my ear as she strives to be heard over the din of a hundred people eating and talking. I shiver and nod.

While Chelsea is gone with her mom and Candace to do whatever it is she has to do to pee in that dress, I scan the massive dining room. My father and my uncles are gathered around one of the tables, done eating and onto plotting. I'm sure they will take over the stage soon. It sits ready for them, the drum set quietly sitting behind the two guitars and one bass, leaned on stands and waiting for the geniuses that will soon make them weep for my guests.

Beyond the stage is a set of grand french doors leading out to a wooden deck overlooking the Bay. Candace's friend, Meg, walks through the doors and back into the room. Behind her Hayden is still on the deck, pacing its length.

I get up and walk to the door, curious about my brother-in-law. As I open the door and the fresh night air hits me, I take a closer look at him.

We've gotten to know each other a little over the past two years. And in all that time, I've never seen Hayden look so anxious. He always seems so laid back and relaxed to me.

"Hey, brother," I say, slapping him on the back.

He grins at me. "Hi, Henry." He shakes my hand for like the third time today. "I'm really am glad you married my baby sister, man. I mean that."

"Thanks." I lean on the railing next to him. "I'm pretty freaking happy about it, too."

"You two are perfect for each other." He says it almost wistfully.

"Is…uh…is everything all right?"

"Huh." He snorts out a half laugh and runs his hand through his hair. "I think I just got myself into something."

"With Meg or your date?" I hoped to hell it wasn't his date. She was a hot mess if I'd ever seen one.

"Meg," he says on a sigh.

"Really?" This surprises me. I happen to know he

and Meg can't stand each other. They are truly opposites. They make even Jack and Candace look like they have a lot in common.

"Not like that." He turns to face me. "You know I hired her to be my secretary, right?"

I nod. The whole family is still trying to figure that one out.

"Well, I think I just hired her to be my matchmaker, too?"

I laugh. "You *think*."

"She's kind of a force to be reckoned with."

"True," I agree. I'd spent enough time with the strong-willed artist to know that.

"She talked me into letting her find me a potential wife. For a fee, of course."

I shake my head as if this will help clear it. "What?" Hayden is a consummate playboy. The idea of him with a wife is a foreign concept.

Then again, the idea of me with a wife was once pretty far-fetched too. I suppress a smile at the thought.

Hayden lets out a long breath. "I need to settle down. I'm the CEO of the company now. I need stability. I can't be running around with girls like Shanda." He gestures toward the dining room. I look through the glass door and see his date riding on the lap of my cousin Danny. She's drunk and horny, and soon to be very disappointed.

"No argument there. She might end up in a fight with Danny's boyfriend."

Hayden laughs.

I turn back to him. "Do you think Meg can do it? Find you a great little woman?" I sound a little irreverent, but I *do* want to know.

Hayden shrugs. "Probably not. But it could be entertaining to let her try. Besides, she obviously needs the money."

I heard Candace and Chelsea talking about this the other day. Something is going on with Meg, but she's being completely tight-lipped about whatever it is. Candace could easily help her out. Hell, Chelsea and I could, too, these days. But she won't hear of it. And now she's turned to Hayden, working for him to earn extra cash.

"Should be interesting."

"Hmmm." He pauses, obviously deep in thought. Then he looks past me through the windows in the french doors. "I think you gotta go, man."

I turn to follow his gaze and see Chelsea. She's standing in the middle of the dance floor alone. My father and my uncle have taken up their spots on stage. All that is missing for the first dance is me.

I race into the room, Hayden at my heels. He turns one way. I turn the other. In a few strides, I have Chelsea gathered up in my arms and my father starts to strum his guitar.

"Sorry I'm late," I say softly.

She shakes her head and smiles. "You're right on time."

We start to move. And Chelsea's grin grows wider. She only discovered I could dance last week. I don't know why she was surprised. I have a million aunts and an over-bearing mom. Surely she had to realize they would have taught me to dance.

She loves my moves.

I rest my forehead against hers as we float fluidly across the floor. My dad's voice is soft and low, creating a backdrop for the movement of our bodies. "Did I tell you how amazing you look today?"

"Yes. A few times, actually."

"And did I mention how badly I want to get you naked?"

She nods, making her forehead rub against mine.

I swing her around and look out at our family and friends. They are all smiling at us, happy we've found each other. My mother is crying again. My sister is laughing, no doubt at the silly, satisfied look on my face. And Hayden looks sad, like he never expects to have what I have.

A word about the author...

Kay Harris has had a diverse career with jobs ranging from college professor to park ranger. Now she adds author to her repertoire. Kay writes romance novels that contain a little bit of sweet, a dash of sexy, a touch of heartbreak, and a whole lot of fun!

Kay grew up in the Midwest and has since lived all over the western United States including Montana, Wyoming, Utah, Arizona, Nevada, and California. She loves to hike, is obsessed with museums, and enjoys taking her extremely tall and very handsome husband on adventures.

http://kayharrisauthor.com